The King and Queen of Moonlight Bay was published in 1982 by Dell. In 2002 it became a Hallmark Channel movie, starring Kristin Bell, Tim Matheson, Sean Young and Edward Asner. This is a revised version of the original novel.

The King and Queen of Moonlight Bay

Alison Dodge hasn't seen her father since she was a child. In the summer of her fifteenth year, she decides that this is her last chance to get to know the man she's only been able to speculate about. She wants to spend the summer with him. He replies that she can, but he doesn't know why she'd want to. He lives on an island. She won't like the life he leads. He attempts to dissuade her. He fails.

The summer is a struggle for both of them. Alison brings her anger at being abandoned to the island with her. Her father, Al Dodge, resists her presence in every way he can. The experiment nearly fails. *The King and Queen of Moonlight Bay* is about two people fighting their way to a relationship.

By Michael de Guzman

Melonhead

Beekman's Big Deal

The Bamboozlers

Finding Stinko

Henrietta Hornbuckle's Circus of Life

Growing up Rita

Cosmos DeSoto
and the Case of the Giant Steel TEETH

Searching for a Place to be

The King and Queen of Moonlight Bay
(Revisited)

Praise for other books

Growing Up Rita

"A life lesson for adults and kids alike, a great read with a quiet message of understanding, friendship and tolerance." -- Peter Pan (London, UK)

Searching for a Place to be

The writing is simple and spare, no wasted words. You're pulled into the story from the very first page, and not let go until the very end --- which brings its own surprises and amazements. His books are aimed at young boys, but the subjects are very adult, most of all in this book; and the way they unfold and how they resolve are suitable for a very wide audience. -- Tsarina

Beekman's Big Deal

"Kids will care about Beekman and Leo, whose relationship is wonderfully close, funny and real. You could say this story is a big deal." -- *Kirkus*

The Bamboozlers

"de Guzman's humorous, snappily paced caper introduces another spunky, credible young hero." -- *Publishers Weekly (Starred)*

Melonhead

"A poignant story of a disconnected boy searching for a place where he feels loved and wanted." -- School Library Journal

The King and Queen of Moonlight
(Revisited)

A novel

Michael de Guzman

Copyright © 1982 by Michael de Guzman
michaeldeguzman.com

All rights, except movie rights, are reserved

This is a work of fiction.

Lyrics from *Moonlight Bay* by Edward Madden & Percy Wenrich: © 1912 Warner Bros. Inc. Copyright renewed. All rights reserved. Used by Permission.

Lyrics from *There'll be Blue Birds Over The White Cliffs of Dover*, by Nat Burton & Walter Kent: Copyright MCMXLI, Renewed by Shapiro, Bernstein & Co., Inc., New York, NY, 10022. Used by permission.

Cover art by Rebecca Bush

ISBN-13: 9781505388855
ISBN-10: 1505388856

1.Father and daughter - fiction. 2. Divorce - fiction. 3. Small town life - fiction. 4. Coming of age - fiction. 5. First sexual experience

For Michelle and Rachel, for their patience and love. What was true then, is true now.

ONE

I watched the clock. The day seemed endless. It had begun at seven thirty when I protested my way out of bed and was now no further along than just past ten. All my days seemed endless. Waiting for my father to answer the letter I'd written him caused the minutes to take hours. The minutes dragged on, seeming to repeat themselves, apparently unable to move beyond the point of their origin. I concentrated my energy on the clock. I willed the large, red second hand to go faster, to spin its way forward so that when I opened my eyes the second day would be done and I could rush home to the mail. But when I opened my eyes it was three seconds later or twelve seconds later, and the stubborn red hand of the clock continued to stutter forward one blasted click after another.

Time always went slowest for me in June and that made it worse. I liked school and did well enough, but by

June it was time for it to be over. My mother, Jane, counseled patience. She thought I had none. I didn't see the need. Everything took too long as it was, and I had no interest in slowing time further by being patient. I'd written my father in May and had waited long enough.

Dear Dodge,
I would like to spend the summer with you. I have thought of many ways to ask about this and have tried to come up with some brilliant scheme to convince you to say yes but finally decided that the best thing was just to ask. So, I'm asking. May I spend the summer with you?

Jane and Horace are going off to Europe on business, then they've taken a house outside London for the month of August. They want me to come but I said no. We won't want to do the same things and I'll just be in the way and in the end we'll all wish I hadn't. They asked me at camp to be a junior counselor but I won't do that either. I'm too old for all that singing around the camp fire and telling ghost stories. So, unless you take me, I have no place to go.

School is out June 15th and I need another week to take care of things around here so I can be ready. Jane and Horace don't leave until the first week of July, but I want to come before then. The sooner the better. I know it must seem strange to you, my asking this when we've spent so little time together, but I've thought about it a lot and about our lives and I think it is important that we get to know each other. After all, I am your daughter.

School has gone well again this year. I have all my usual grades. I haven't grown at all, not taller anyway, but I guess I'm tall enough. Robert, the doorman, retired last month and they had a party for him in the lobby and gave him a suitcase. He told me he had no place to go. I hope you will give this letter very serious consideration. I've thought about it for a long time and it's very important to me. I hope you are well. I hope to hear from you very soon. Please.

Love,

Alison

P.S. I know I would love your house and your island and that we would get along fine and have great fun.

"I wish you'd waited. I wish you'd talked it over with us first. I don't think it's a good idea. It's not a good idea at all." My mother spoke to me about the letter with a passion I didn't know she possessed. I told her about it the day after I mailed it, and she was crimson with unhappiness.

"I'm sorry to have to say this, but the man never did anything for anyone but himself his whole life. You're someone else to think about, and he doesn't like to think about anyone but himself." Jane was unrelenting in her opposition to the prospect of my visit, to the idea that I would spend any time at all with Dodge. "He's selfish. He's petty. He's mean." She said she meant well. She said she was trying to protect me. She said she was trying to prepare me for whatever disappointments would be forthcoming from her former husband, for as sure as the sun sat in the sky, he would break my heart.

I listened to each word and tried to filter out the bitterness. I tried always to do that because I had learned that much of what my mother presented as fact was opinion born of fear or anger or pain or all three. We argued a good deal when I was fifteen and it disturbed us both and we attempted to establish rules. We would listen to each other without comment and when we responded it would be done without raised voices, without becoming emotional. That morning I broke the rules. I screamed at her.

"He can't be more selfish and mean and petty than you're being right now. He can't be." She collected herself and left the room.

To my mother time was now. It was something you held in your hand and had control of. The only purpose served by the past and future was what they brought to the present. Her feelings about my father came to the surface, became part of the moment now, because I wanted to spend time with him. I knew when I mailed the letter that she would bring a great unhappiness to it. I almost didn't mail it because of that. But I was fifteen.

When I was about to become thirteen, she took me aside for a talk about the female body and its functions. "Your period is nothing more and nothing less than a normal female body function. You should be aware of your body. you should understand and appreciate it. Perhaps you'd like to ask some questions. That might be productive." She lighted a cigarette and leaned back and waited for me to test the information she'd read the night before.

"I got my period a few months ago." I couldn't think of any other way to say it. I smiled hopefully. Jane crushed out her cigarette, paced for a moment, muttered something I couldn't understand and left the room. That was the first big lesson I learned about communicating with my mother.

I was sorry afterward that I hadn't shared the event of my period. I simply hadn't thought to do so. It seemed to me that my mother was absolutely correct, it was nothing more than a normal body function. I'd read about it and talked about it with my doctor when I went for the school physical and dealt with it when it happened. It hadn't seemed necessary to make an announcement. After Jane's reaction to my period it didn't seem at all wise to discuss with her the first boy who kissed me on the lips and tried to jam his tongue in my mouth, nor to mention in any way the first boy who tried to get his hand up my dress.

I continued to watch the clock that day in school and for all those days, and I listened to my teachers droning on and on. I thought about those first boys in my life. I kissed most of the boys who took me out and had done some heavy necking and let one boy unbutton my blouse. I remember fondly the first boy who ever tried to feel me up. We were necking on the couch in his living room, and he moved his hand from the back of my shoulder to an area near my chest where I could see it hovering like some misplaced object in search of a home. I watched that quivering butterfly until it clamped down against my chest approximately where my left breast was supposed to be. My breast was there, and the fact that the young man's hand missed its mark was more a function of his nervousness than my lack of development. I was budding then. In any event, the hand stayed where it was, rigid in its anxiety. We continued to kiss wetly and he made moaning noises and I felt his hand, from time to time, squeeze down on itself. I didn't tell my mother about him.

I didn't tell my mother about the young man who tried to get his hand up my dress in the backseat of a taxi on the way home from a school dance. She waited up for me that night to ask what everyone wore and what the decorations were like and for me to tell her about the young man who'd taken me. I did not tell her how I'd first felt his fingers on my knee and then felt them crawl up my thigh in search of what lay beyond. I hit him with a closed fist and told him to keep his hands to himself. The young man looked frantically to the front and folded his arms tightly across his chest, only to find himself staring at the driver, who had nearly snapped his neck off turning to see what happened. I did rather well not to laugh out loud just then.

The letter from my father finally arrived. It was there one day when I came home from school. I held it gingerly and took it to my room.

Alison,
You may come for the summer, but I wonder why you want to. My place and the way I live are rough. I get along without the things you are used to. You should think twice before finally deciding. I will certainly understand if you change your mind.

If you do come, take the train to Kingston on the 25th. Let me know when the train arrives and I will meet you. I drive a red pickup truck. Let me know your decision.

15

Dodge

I read the letter and read it again and never did I see in it the message that I wasn't wanted. I saw only the first six words, "You may come for the summer..." All I knew was that I hadn't been rejected.

TWO

Sandy Bateman hesitated for a moment, haunched above Dodge like a pale bird in the dark, then rolled over onto her back and grinned. “It was nice,” she said.

“Better than nice,” he said.

“It was good.” She was teasing him now.

Dodge pushed himself up on an elbow. “Better,” he said.

“Okay, better,” she said.

“If you say so,” Dodge said. He wanted a drink. He’d wanted one all night. Sandy had agreed to go out with him if he promised not to touch a drop. Now he regretted it. His daughter was coming tomorrow. It seemed some sort of dream, as though it were happening to someone else. After a decade of living alone his life was about to be infringed upon. He didn’t want to change any aspect of how he lived. He wasn’t sure he could. He was being put upon; he was permitting himself to be put upon, and he didn’t know why. He said yes when he could have said no.

No was what he meant. No was what he wanted to write her back. He wanted a drink.

It was late and Middleport was closed for the evening. Sandy's apartment was the upstairs of a two-family house. It was back off Smith Street on a lane that ended at the edge of the south cove. It was away from things. She'd picked it because it was private and because it was bare and she'd been able to decorate it to satisfy her own tastes. It was the first time in her life that she'd been able to do that.

They had drinks in the kitchen afterward. Sandy's idea. She couldn't stand to see him suffer. It was late. One drink wouldn't hurt anything. One drink and he had to go because she had to get up early for work. He wanted to talk about his daughter and she wanted to let him. She liked Dodge. She liked pleasing him. She didn't always understand why. He had a nasty temper sometimes and a low opinion of himself and wasn't always decent company. But when he was feeling good, on those rare occasions, he was terrific.

Dodge was not the future, not for her. He had none of his own, and he wasn't going to deny her the slim chance she had for hers. For the present he was fine. He was a good lover and he could make her laugh sometimes and she needed that desperately. Sometimes her life threatened to suffocate her. She married out of high school and followed her husband and, in the horrible vacuum of a strange Midwestern town, she was brutalized and abandoned. Now she worked for her father, and the store would be hers someday if she wanted to spend the rest of her life in Middleport.

18

She looked at the man at the kitchen table and knew that at least part of her was lying. She did care for him. As he poured his heart out about his daughter and his doubts about having her spend the summer with him she realized she was listening to a frightened man. He was an odd one, Al Dodge, a man not easily understood. He did not altogether fit into the scheme of things in Middleport, certainly not into the mainstream of things. He was still an outsider. He made little effort to accommodate others and participated only as it suited his moods. He was not an open or forthcoming man. He played in the Labor Day softball game but did nothing else by the way of civic activity. He asked for nothing.

What the people of Middleport thought of Dodge was uncertain. His ten years in the village had given him a place. It wasn't enough to make him a native, but it was enough for the natives to acknowledge his presence without raising questions. They knew he lived on the margin of things. They knew he was good craftsman and that he gave an honest job for the pay he asked. Some of them knew he had a daughter in New York who'd never been to their village. Most of them liked him more than they disliked him, and the assumption was that he was with them to stay.

Dodge left Sandy's and drove to the dock and rowed across the channel. It was late and the houses were dark, blacked-out forms against a partially moonlit sky. The oars cut into the water, making small splashing sounds as they went in and came out. The oarlocks clicked to the tune of Dodge's effort. The boat bumped finally against his small dock and he tied up. The night was quiet. The creatures of his domain were at rest. He stood for a while on the rickety walkway that extended out a few feet past the low-tide mark and contemplated his domain.

Twenty feet in front of him was his house, his house of stone. When he got it, it was falling down. It had been used as a place to drink and smoke and fornicate by anyone with the means to get there. When he first saw it, people and weather and time had all done their share of destruction. All the windows were broken. Rubbish was piled high about the place. The inside had been scarred by vandals, who had written obscenely upon the walls. When Dodge went to Sarah Conway she was pleased to let him live in the place for nothing if he'd fix it up and look after it and the one acre of scrub land surrounding it. He moved in and learned as he went, making many mistakes, working until he was done, and in the process he'd learned enough about fixing things to make his living as a handyman. He created a house that provided warmth and protection. The aesthetics of it were not a concern, then or now. The first half dozen confrontations with intruders left the island free to Dodge and the raccoons and woodchucks and fiddler crabs and birds.

The house was made of brick and stone and had a sloping roof with a single dormer. There were four widows and a door across the front. There was a door in back and a window in the dormer that looked out over the channel. Dodge used old stones and old bricks and concrete to make the house tight. He replaced glass and put in a coal stove and a kerosene heater. He repaired the small dock and bought the skiff and caulked it. He rowed a great deal and it showed in his shoulders and back. He was muscular from the rowing and from digging quahogs with twenty-foot tongs. That was a merciless operation for a night's dinner, and among the few people in the world for whom he felt compassion were those who made their living at it. Again and again and again the metal jaws at the end of the twenty-foot wooden poles were lowered into the water to the muck at the bottom and worked back and forth until they got pulled up the twenty feet to the surface. The muck was gone through and the broken glass and beer cans and seaweed and empty razor clam shells were sorted out and thrown back. If a quahog or two was to be found after all that, it was a successful haul. Then you did it again, hour after hour, from dawn of the day till its end, every day until you were too old to do it at all.

Dodge was now a professional odds-and-ends man. He painted kitchens and signs for businesses and the outside of houses. He did odd jobs of carpentry and brick masonry and garden work and roof repair. He did a bit of almost everything to make the few dollars that were necessary to eating, drinking, and keeping his life together. It didn't take much. The house, the boat, the truck, a few changes of clothes, his tools, these had been paid for and were all now maintained at minimal cost. The piano had been purchased at Pop's, the used furniture store on old Route One. For fifteen dollars. It had cost him another forty dollars to get it fixed, another twenty-five to get it across to the island, and another twenty-five to get it tuned. Five men had accompanied the piano in a fishing boat at high tide. They'd lifted it gently and carried it with care, and now it sat upright against a wall of the large room that was the downstairs of his house. The stacks of old sheet music had been cheap. When he bought them, people were still giving such things away.

Dodge's island, as some in town had started calling it, was an acre of sand, rock, slat grass, bush, and scrub pine trees. The far side of it was separated from the mainland by a waterway that could hardly be called more than a stream. At high tide it was perhaps fifteen feet wide and navigable by punt. It was wildly overgrown on both the island and mainland sides, which afforded as much protection and isolation as the wide channel at the island's other side. The island was a place to eat and drink and read and play the piano and sing old songs and get drunk and be alone. That's what he'd wanted when he abandoned New York and his family. It was what he had.

Directly in back of the house was the well that supplied fresh water. It was deep and worked from a hand pump. The water sometimes got brackish. A pipe went from the well to the kitchen, where another hand pump made it possible to get water without going outside. There were days when the pump in the kitchen produced no water at all. There was also a cistern for collecting rainwater.

There was no electricity on the island. Dodge kept a gasoline generator he'd found on the island in repair, but it was never used. He used kerosene lamps and candles. There was no telephone on the island. If you wanted to reach him, you saw him in town or left a note in his mailbox, or you left word with Sandy at the hardware store.

Behind Dodge's house was an outhouse. It was six feet high, a rectangular structure of wood whose door wouldn't close all the way and whose boards grinned the gaps that winter's abuse had imposed upon them. It got so cold in the outhouse at times of year that Dodge thought for sure he'd freeze to death before he finished his errand.

Dodge looked a moment longer at his world and recognized within himself some sense of satisfaction that he'd been able to make it his. He walked slowly to the house and inside put match to wick and watched the kerosene lamp sputter and smoke and finally make steady flame. He fetched a bottle from the cabinet above the sink, broke the seal, and with a glass took it to the piano where he started to play and think about tomorrow. What the hell was he going to do with a fifteen-year-old kid for a whole summer? He started playing louder and started to sing about voices humming and banjos strumming and about the girl he left behind, down on Moonlight Bay.

THREE

"Alison."

My mother brought me back from my speculations about Middleport. I saw her staring at me. She and Horace were seated at each end of the dining room table and I was between them. There were candles and lace and a good bottle of wine. They'd permitted me a glass which I'd not yet touched. It was a special dinner, my special dinner. I was leaving in the morning for my summer with Dodge. I scooped up a forkful of peas and smiled at my mother and was aware of the pained attempt at a smile I received in return. Jane sighed and went back to her eating. I returned to my thoughts.

The past week had been miserable. With each passing day my anxiety increased until I was nearly bursting with it. Surely my portrait of Middleport was a misplaced fantasy. Surely my portrait of Dodge and his world was idealized so far beyond reality that I would be disappointed no matter how they turned out. I had studied intently the one photograph I had of Dodge and me. It showed us together at the Central Park Zoo by the elephant cage. I was nine then and not particularly attractive. We stood stiffly in the chill, side by side, looking straight into the camera. I remembered a good deal about the day of the photograph but almost nothing about the man at my side. Looking at it, I tried to decipher what kind of person my father was. I called him Dodge and had done so since his first visit to see me after he left us. He made a deal with me then. "Call me Dodge and I'll call you Alison. It's much more grown-up than Daddy and daughter." It was a fine game and I enjoyed it for many years. I wasn't so certain about it when I was fifteen. I looked up at my mother again. The letter from my father saying I could come had driven her nearly to despair.

"It's exactly what I said," she said when she saw it. "He doesn't want you. He can't say no because he's your father, but he doesn't want you. It couldn't be more clear. All you have to do is read it to know that." She was frantic. "You can't go. It's quite obvious that you can't go. It's out of the question."

I stood my ground. "He said I could and I'm going to." We were in my bedroom. It was a crucial moment. "My father said I could spend the summer with him and I'm going to. He is my father."

She took my hands and held them tightly and looked at me for the longest time. I knew she was angry. I knew she wanted to forbid me. I knew she wanted to find the words that would make me change my mind. That moment seemed to last forever. I wanted desperately to help her. But I would not. I could not. Going to my father hurt my mother. I was aware of that. I was causing a complication in everyone's life, upsetting Jane and Horace and Dodge because of what seemed to them a whim.

"You go to your father," was what she finally said to me. "You should spend the summer with him and have the best time of your life." She kissed me then and squeezed my hands again and left my room, to go to hers to cry.

The next day Jane began her involvement with my preparations. She insisted on it. She made lists and bought things and started to sew name tags into them. I screamed at her that I was not going to camp. We argued about that and about what I would bring, and one day when I came home from school we had the first real full-blown fight of our lives. On the floor of my room was a steamer trunk with stacks of clothing surrounding it and my mother taking inventory.

"You'll need everything I've laid out." She worked as she talked. "You'll need shorts and T-shirts, three bathing suits, in case one gets ripped, your camp sweatshirts, two pairs of sneakers..." She took a breath in mid-sentence and I exploded.

"For God's sake Mother, I don't need all that. I don't need half of it." I let out all the frustration and anxiety I'd been storing up. "Why can't you mind your own business! I'm not a child. Get out of my room. I'll manage myself. I'll pack myself."

Jane stood and started from the room. She mumbled, "I just wanted to help," and went to the door. She turned back. "I don't want you to go." I'm sure it nearly killed her to say so. "I can't help myself. I'm sorry. I just don't want you to go. It's a mistake. A terrible mistake. Please, Alison, spend the summer with us. Please."

I was mean then and still angry and too young to understand in any measure what was going on inside my mother. I attacked her weakness. "You don't want me to go because it's my father. What are you afraid of? That I might like him? That I might like him better than you?"

"That's not fair. It's not what I mean."

"What do you mean?"

"I won't go to Europe." She brightened suddenly at this new idea. "I'll stay. Horace can go alone and you and I will spend summer together. Just the two of us. It'll be such fun, Alison. We'll go to shows and concerts. We'll explore New York like a couple of out-of-towners, like a couple of pals. I've always wanted to do that." She paused, out of breath, her expression hopeful. I cried out for her but it was inside and it stayed there. "I'm going to spend the summer with my father," is what I said.

"Are you punishing me for something?" She appeared wild-eyed. "What did I ever do to you to make you treat me like this?"

I wanted to explain. I wanted her to know how I felt. But I didn't know myself. I could only repeat myself. "I'm going to spend the summer with my father."

Jane was angry at Dodge. She didn't trust him because he'd abandoned her. He was irresponsible and that was the greatest sin one could commit. She admitted to me that she loved him once. She described him as handsome in a slightly flawed way. He was attractive to her and to many women, and he was moderately successful in business and there was the promise of more. They enjoyed life when they first met. They lived well, Jane told me. Theatre, dinner out, weekend trips, that was the way of things for them before I was born. But it went wrong before I appeared. Jane took great pains to assure me of that, that I was not the cause of their problems. The history of their failure followed its inevitable course. That was her explanation. It was external. The signals came from the outside world. The wife of Dodge's boss had taken her to lunch one day to caution her about Dodge's changed attitude at work. Dodge was liked. They wanted him to do well. She had to help him get back on track. A company wife could do that much and more to assist a good man. After my birth, Jane's focus on life changed. I became it. When my father changed jobs then changed again, she expressed little concern. She was absorbed with being a mother and ignored everything and everyone else. It was her escape from things unpleasant, her defense, and it worked until one day when it didn't, when I was five years old, when my father left and didn't return.

She could still muster feelings, the disbelief, the anger, the fear that consumed her. My father left and he set the terms of his leaving. He left me to Jane. He left everything he had, all his insurance, the cash, the property, everything, and took only a suitcase of clothes and a few hundred dollars. There was no one for my mother to talk with about it. She didn't understand the concept of professional help. It was private business and one didn't discuss that with outsiders. There was money for a year and there was a certain style and dignity to maintain. That was how Jane saw the situation. I would continue with private school. She would find a new husband. She never forgave my father that one great indignity. She had to find a new provider without time to do so properly. My mother had no training and she refused to get a job as a sales clerk at Bloomingdale's where she'd see her friends, even if such a job was possible for her. She hated Dodge for forcing her to find a man. The man was Horace, and for a long time her anger at Dodge was taken out on him.

I looked up at my mother across the dinner table that last night before my summer began and saw that she was deep in thought. I looked over at Horace and saw, that for the moment, he was occupied with himself as well. It was a dinner without joy. They'd given me presents before sitting down at the table, a gold chain with a gold A on it and a new wallet with two hundred and fifty dollars in new bills in it and a photograph of the two of them with a message of love on it. They gave me a pen and a packet of stationary and their itinerary so I'd know where to write them and not have any excuse not to. I accepted it all with quiet thanks though I wanted to give the money back. It was less trouble to keep it. The meal was eaten mostly in silence. Horace tried a half dozen times without success to get something by way of conversation started. It was obvious that he didn't like the idea of my spending the summer with Dodge any better than Jane did, but he tried to make the best of it. He told my mother that it would go well and that I should be sent off with the memory of their smiling faces. They could not stand in the way. If they did, I'd resent it, and in the end that would cause more harm to our relationship than the summer away.

Horace told me that I had a responsibility to be patient with Jane. He wanted me to see her point of view and to understand that I was going off with their blessing even though it was difficult. I said I understood. I thought I did. I'm certain now I didn't at all.

"We'll go early to the station tomorrow and have breakfast. I always enjoyed breakfast at railway stations when I was young. There's something about all those people coming and going. I used to sit in railway stations for hours trying to figure out where they were going and what kind of people they were." Horace spoke all that with such passion that he arrested my attention and Jane's and we stared at him with wonder. He smiled at my mother, then at me, and we both smiled back.

"I'd like to have breakfast at the station," I said at once. "It sounds wonderful."

"It is and that's exactly what we'll do." He took Jane's hand in his. "We'll all eat as much as we want and we'll watch the people and we'll try to figure out what we can about the way of the world."

FOUR

The train left the tunnel and made its way toward the 125th Street Station. I wrapped myself into a window seat, my legs tucked up under me. The seat next to me was filled with magazines and a book and my handbag. I was glad to be out of the tunnel. I feared getting stuck in its terrible darkness.

The streets below and the scattered wash that hung from lines and windows and the tiny black fragments of people moving about registered indelibly. I could see faces peering out from apartments at the passing train. I saw my face reflected in the window of the train, a worried, frightened face. I shifted my attention back to the outside world and wondered about the people who lived here. I wondered how they spent their time. I wondered what they wondered about. I wished I knew some black people. I wished I wasn't afraid of them.

When the train pulled into the station, I saw the flat, hostile eyes of more black people. I stared out the window at them then turned away. I was certain I would share their anger if I were one of them. I too would stare at a white girl on a train with hatred in my heart and eyes. We left the 125th Street Station and headed to cross the river and I felt the tension leaving my body. I was ashamed of that. I thought instead of the morning just passed at Pennsylvania Station.

At breakfast, Horace told me stories of trips he'd made by train when he was young. He spoke lovingly of a kind of railroad that didn't exist anymore and of dining cars that used real linen and silver and crystal and good china and served food that was the equal of a first class restaurant.

"Railway stations used to be grand places." Horace smiled a faraway smile when he told me that. He sipped his coffee and let his mind wander and came back to me a few moments later. "There was a restaurant in the station at Cleveland that was a wonder. It had a ceiling so high you hurt your neck when you looked up at it. There was glass up there and there were dark corners and it looked and smelled like a restaurant in a railway station was supposed to smell. It wasn't a bus station or a drugstore. It was a railway station. The people who waited on you had all worked there forever. They were fastidious in their concern. They served a roast beef like you've never tasted before in your life. Melt in your mouth." He savored the memory. He looked about at Pennsylvania Station and sighed for his childhood.

My mother said nothing all during breakfast. She was unhappy and incapable of not letting it show. Horace carried the burden of being cheerful. He was full of suggestions.

"Check carefully before you use the bathroom on the train. Knock twice. I remember an instance when I wasn't paying attention, I knocked once and opened the door at the same time and came face to face with a woman sitting on the toilet with a black girdle down around her knees. She should have locked the door and I was only seven, but she screamed and I screamed and slammed the door and ran into the next car and never came back except for my bag. So knock twice." He laughed. I laughed too, and it pleased him to be the cause of it.

He bought me some magazines and continued talking about trains. "I traveled a lot on them when I was much younger than you. Of course, it was different then. It was a safe way for a child to travel alone. You could talk to anyone. People kept an eye on you. The conductors were big solid men in shiny dark uniforms with vests and hats and gold watch chains. They told you about trains and you got off where you were supposed to get off and they helped you with your stuff. Not that you can't talk to people today. You can. On a train you can. You just have to be careful. Use your judgement." I nodded the whole time he talked and my response satisfied him. When he finished the silence returned. When it became awkward he started up again.

"Eating on a train is the most fun I ever had as a kid. You could spend hours sitting there watching the country fly by while you were having a meal. When you ordered you wrote out what you wanted on a ticket. There was a man who came through ringing a chime, announcing that the dining car was now serving. When you got there they showed you to a seat and gave you a menu and one of those tickets to fill out. It was wonderful." He took a moment to enjoy his own recollection then continued.

"Sometimes I'd get on a train that didn't have a dining car. The late trains and the real locals didn't have them. Men would come aboard with boxes of sandwiches and cold drinks and magazines and newspapers and candy and chewing gum and cigarettes and move through the cars yelling about them and selling them. I never saw people with so much change in their pockets as those men. I never tasted anything in this world as good as one of those stale cheese sandwiches on white bread that wouldn't bend. I never drank anything as good as the warm orange drink they dispensed in those frayed cardboard containers. Late at night when you're a kid traveling alone and hungry and full of yourself, there is nothing better than that."

As we stood by the gate waiting for the announcement to board, Jane finally spoke. She spoke softly. She found it difficult to look at me. "I'm sorry," she said. Horace busied himself. I looked at Jane, knowing what she was going to say, wanting her to know that I knew it so she didn't have to. "I want you to have a good time." She tried to smile and almost managed it. "The things I said, I didn't mean them, not the way they came out."

"That's okay."

"No it's not. Whatever feelings I have about your father have nothing to do with you."

The announcement for my train boomed about us. The gate opened and Horace took my suitcase. My mother hugged me suddenly and quickly let me go. She was starting to cry. She said, "I love you." I think she said it. People were moving about us then and I was never sure.

I watched New York turn into Connecticut and took off my jacket. Jane had bought me a suit for the occasion of my journey and a handbag and shoes to match, and it all made me look older than fifteen. When she first saw me in it she bit her lip and said she wasn't sure she could deal with a grown-up daughter. She'd also given me a letter to give to my father. I opened it. It was a directive, filled with admonitions about how to treat her daughter. It made me sad that she'd written such a thing. I felt myself starting to cry and ripped it up. I would have to work things out for myself. It would be hard enough without a set of instructions on how to wash and feed me. We were moving closer to the shore and Long Island Sound was visible. It was Saturday and the train was a local and it had many stops to make before I reached Middleport.

A boat engine backfired in the channel outside Dodge's house, and the sound of it became a dim chime in the rising tide of his consciousness. He was waking up. He didn't want to wake up. He didn't have to. He tried to recapture the place where he had just been. He could still feel the warmth of it. He could recall the sweet comfort of it. He reached out. Silently he cried out. It seemed such a short journey back to sleep.

If he could remember the dream he'd been having, he could rejoin it where it had abandoned him. If he could find the beginning of the dream, he could start it over and this time slow it down and ride it into the day. He tried to reconstruct it. He saw Fenway Park and saw that it was filled and heard the people. They were hanging from the rafters. They were leaning out the windows of the buildings nearby. They were on roof tops. They were crowded out in the parking lot with their radios. They filled neighborhood bars and complained to each other about the television reception over the heads of endless glasses of draft beer. Their beloved Red Sox were doing battle with the ever hateful New York Yankees. Newspaper headlines flashed by: DO OR DIE! THERE'S NO TOMORROW! ALL THE MARBLES ON THE LINE! It was the last game of the season. Six months of baseball had come down to this one last game. The winner would go on to the World Series. The loser would have to WAIT UNTIL NEXT YEAR!

Dodge was a Red Sox. He was a hard-hitting right fielder with good range, adequate speed, and a splendid arm. He was a steady performer who was good in the clutch, a good hit-and-run man, a good man to break up a double play. He was popular. He was on a bubble gum card. He owned a half interest in a seafood restaurant in Providence, Rhode Island. It had his name on it. One winter, after his best season, he earned an extra $7,750 on the rubber-chicken circuit. Dodge played in the outfield with Ted Williams and Dom DiMaggio.

Now he was in the locker room. He was the last man dressed. He could hear Fenway rocking with the sound of his name. "Dodge! Dodge! Dodge!" they chanted, thousands of them. They yelled and clapped and stamped their feet. He grabbed his glove and started for the field. He reached the dugout and climbed the steps and ran out onto the field, and something in excess of thirty thousand people rose to their feet in appreciation.

The boat backfired again, and Dodge realized that it was not the baseball dream he'd been having. He liked the dream, but it wasn't the one and it wasn't going to work. He ran his tongue over his teeth and shivered. He smacked his lips and tasted the bilge in his mouth and thought about spitting it out and forgot and swallowed instead and swore. He'd started drinking the night before with Sandy. She threw him out after a couple because he became a pain in the ass. Afterward he'd come back to his place to continue drinking. He'd played the piano and sung his songs, every song he knew. He tried to remember how many songs he knew. He started counting them then stopped when he realized he was counting some of the same ones more than once. The only songs he cared about had all been written before 1945. He knew dozens of them, maybe hundreds

His hand ached. His lips were cracked. His tongue felt swollen. He felt a tremendous craving for something he couldn't define. He was angry. It was destructive the way he drank when he was upset. He was aware of his breath suddenly, and he tried to draw away from it. He stank. He felt dirty. He swiped at the air that sat on his face like an abandoned cobweb and missed. He swiped at it again and realized there was nothing there. He wiped his face with a filthy hand and regretted it. He felt terrible. He changed positions, exploring the bed for some comfort that didn't exist. He belched. He farted. He thought about the day ahead and Sandy being angry at him and being almost fifty and having to pick up Alison at the station and the boat backfired again and he woke up.

37

He stood naked next to his bed and surveyed the scene in front of him and tried to feel good about the idea of cleaning his house. He'd started it a half-dozen times before this morning and put it off each time, feeling perhaps that it would go away if he ignored it.

He sat at the kitchen table and counted the cigarette burns on its top, then surveyed his house again. Downstairs it was a single large room that was nearly a perfect rectangle. His bed was against the wall near the kitchen. The piano was against the wall across from that. There was a couch and several stuffed chairs that had once been amply filled with stuffing and that had once all been the same color. They had faded at different rates and were now three shades of green. They were bunched together near the large kerosene heater in the middle of the room. The kitchen was separated from everything else by a counter. Behind it was a sink, the table with two chairs, a coal burning cooking stove and two cabinets. Across from the kitchen, on the far wall, was a stairway that led to the loft that was a third of the area of downstairs. The loft was to be Alison's room for the summer. She'd have privacy. She'd be away from him. He'd carted an old three drawer-dresser up there and had put up a mirror because Sandy told him he had to, and he'd set up a mattress and box spring. It was more comfortable and better looking than anything he'd ever done for himself. It was more trouble than he'd ever gone to for himself. He thought, looking at it, that he might move up there after summer.

Cleaning the house was another matter. It was a mess. It was a pig sty. Sitting with his morning coffee he was perfectly willing to admit it. He was willing to admit that he didn't care. He couldn't see out the windows unless he stood right up to them and squinted through the dirt. The stone floor beneath his feet was caked solid with dirt. Everything sat under a blanket of encrusted dust except the piano and the parts of the kitchen he used with regularity. Sitting there he decided that he'd make his bed and do the best he could with the rest of it. He poured himself another cup of coffee and contemplated where he might begin.

The windows did not open easily. They had to be forced and carefully at that, because the frames were old and fragile and no longer familiar with their function. Dodge knew how to do it and did, but it required as much patience as he owned. When he was done he felt like having a drink and taking the rest of the day off. He aired out the house, after washing the windows, and took a cloth to everything and swept the floor until the broom broke. He cursed the tool and threw it out the door and poured himself a drink and tasted it. He poured the whiskey into a hot cup of coffee and sat and contemplated his labors. He was satisfied. It was enough. It was more than enough. He tasted the laced coffee and thought about picking up Alison and remembered a piece of his own childhood.

He remembered rejection. He was not popular as a child or as a teenager or as a young adult. He laughed out loud when he realized that he wasn't popular now. He tried to fix a clear image of what he'd looked like at some point. He remembered going to dancing school when he was in grammar school for ten cents a lesson. He remembered being selected from time to time to step out into the middle of the gymnasium with some girl or other to demonstrate a step. It was always a basic step. He'd get to do the box step or the L step or some other simple thing, then sit down, flushed with embarrassment, angry at himself, impotent to move, to ask a girl to dance with him on his own. If it hadn't been for dancing school, if it hadn't been for that occasional demonstration, he'd probably have never danced at all.

Dodge decided to allow himself the pleasure of wallowing. He didn't often journey back to his youth. He tasted the coffee and thought about the first girl he'd ever had sex with. She was not pretty. She was not popular. It hadn't mattered because he was neither of those things himself. She returned his feelings without question. She thought him worth being with. Recognition of that had brought momentary joy, and he'd never forgotten it. They spent hours together and days and weeks, walking and talking, holding hands eventually, suffering the abuse of their peers for behaving in so absurd a way. Then they began exploring and experimenting with each other. There was fear and anxiety and anticipation mixed into a kind of out-of-focus excitement as they took off their clothes and heaped them into a mattress. They touched and kissed and held each other and in time they made the love of adolescents.

Dodge smiled at the memory of it. They had convinced each other that afternoon that they'd achieved ecstasy. They held each other as tightly as they could until they knew it was time to go home. When they let go, they realized they'd achieved something they didn't want, something they couldn't help. They sensed in each other an aspect of human failure. There was no happiness in what they'd done. Dodge knew later, when he reached some understanding of himself and the world, that such feelings were tragically misplaced. But then they'd parted with an unspoken understanding that they'd violated something sacred. They felt shame, and whenever they saw each other after that there was a spasm of pain reflected in their eyes. It served to increase his awkwardness and sense of isolation from people. It eventually led him to understand how senselessly cruel people were to each other, especially to their young.

He remembered the girl but not her name. He wished for a fleeting moment that he could write her and tell her that everything was all right. He sipped his coffee and hoped that she was happy and well, then realized that she'd been the age Alison was now. He'd once made love to a girl who was his daughter's age.

The train's movement and sound mesmerized me and in that pleasant state I tried to conjure up what feelings I had about my father. His visits to New York had always been fun. We got along easily. The time we'd spent together had always gone well. I took the photograph from my handbag and studied it and remembered other times. I remembered movies we'd seen and places we we'd gone for dinner. Our conversations were always busy with word games and observations about people and places. Our days together were always full, highly organized, with almost no time in them for anything personal. I realized, looking at the man in the wrinkled suit, that I didn't know whether I liked him or not. He seemed a nice man. He seemed that way. I didn't know.

Love was another matter to be considered, and I did that as the train rattled on through Connecticut. I wondered a lot about love. There were so many different kinds to contemplate. There was love of self. I'd been taught the importance of that in school. You couldn't love anyone else unless you loved yourself. There was love of friends. There was love of pets. There was love of a husband, of another person who was more than a friend. There was love of parents. I hadn't experienced any of them yet. I'd not yet loved and been loved in return, not with the unthinking, unreserved passion one was supposed to experience, that I hoped one experienced. I didn't feel that kind of love for Jane and Horace. I felt guilty about that but could do nothing to alter what was a fact. I'd never had a pet beyond an occasional goldfish whose passing, while troubling, was marked by an absence of emotion. I hadn't yet had a husband or lover. I had friends, but none that evoked strong emotion in me. I felt nothing at all about my father because there was nothing to feel beyond my growing sense of anxiety. I looked at the photograph and didn't know at all what to feel for the man in it. I experienced a rush of confusion. My own identity became a problem. I looked at the window as we moved past an abandoned factory and saw my face. A stranger looked back at me. I felt hunger and ran from my problem to the dining car.

Dodge inspected his wardrobe. The word made him laugh. Once he'd had suits and sport jackets and flannel trousers and drawers filled with soft shirts and socks and underwear and a dozen pairs of shoes on the floor of his closet. He'd given it all away when he left New York. What he had now were three pairs of work pants, three denim shirts, a heavy cable knit sweater with a hole in it, a heavy jacket, a corduroy sport jacket with fake leather buttons, and two pairs of shoes —work boots and moccasins. The old gabardine suit hung unused in a dry cleaning bag in the back of the closet. He wore socks and underwear in winter and neither in summer. It didn't take him long to survey the wonder of all this and to decide what to wear. He put on the best of the work pants and the best of the shirts, his corduroy jacket and his moccasins. He had a sudden urge to look at himself. He had to go up to the loft to do it.

It wasn't possible for Dodge to stand straight to see himself in the mirror. The ceiling was too low where he'd put it. He hoped that Alison hadn't grown too much. With his knees bent he absorbed this image and, pleased, turned to take in what was going to be his daughter's room. The dormer window looked out over the channel, and he thought it was a nice view. The window could be opened, and that would make for a nice breeze at night. It would be good sleeping up here. The bed, the dresser, the kerosene lamp and the candle in its glass bowl on top of the wooden milk carton next to the bed made a nice picture. He was momentarily pleased with himself. Getting the mice and spiders and the wasp's nest out of the loft wasn't easy. He'd made it into a good place to live. He turned back to the mirror for another moment of satisfaction and found it.

He rowed across the channel and tied up and made for the truck. He was nervous but assured in his own mind that he'd done the best he could. It would go well. Why wouldn't it go well? She was his daughter. He was an adult and she was a child. He'd go about his business, and she'd settle into the routine and meet a few people her own age and go to the beach and go back to New York. There was nothing to be concerned about. He started the truck and let it warm up. He adjusted the mirror and smiled at himself and wet his hand and pasted back a piece of hair that was sticking up, then put the truck in first gear and started for the station.

It wasn't a dining car at all but a snack car. It was a great disappointment to me not to be able to sit at a table and live for myself the experience Horace described in such great and colorful detail. It was not to be. Even the cheese sandwich was a disappointment. It came in clear plastic wrap and had no taste at all. It wasn't even stale.

I decided, while I was eating the sandwich, that life was a long series of small disappointments. You read about something or were told about something and you imagined how it would be and when you tried it you were inevitably disappointed. Why wasn't the realization of a thing at all close to the expectation of it?

The train stopped at Old Saybrook and I wondered why a place had such a name. New London I understood. New York I understood. Westerly was next. Then Kingston. I'd already made arrangements with the conductor to help me with my suitcase when I got there. I had nothing to do now but watch Connecticut turn into

Rhode Island and deal with my increasingly nervous stomach. I asked the conductor how long it would be then went to the bathroom. I just barely remembered to knock twice before trying the door.

Dodge sat at the bar at Rudy's Rest sipping a beer. He thought a beer or two wouldn't hurt anything. He thought it would help. Besides, he was early. Rudy's was on Route One near where it intersected with the road he'd have to take to the station. It was a disreputable looking building that was mostly passed by because it didn't look right. It was a first class bar and Rudy was a first class man to spend time with. It was the best place to spend time on this road, better by far than the big plastic places that had opened up in recent years to cater to the college crowd. It would take ten minutes to get to the station from Rudy's. He checked his watch and looked over at Rudy who was doing the crossword. They were the only ones in the place at eleven thirty in the morning.

"How many different kinds of bars you been in?" Rudy asked it while fetching a glass from the cooler and filling it with beer from the tap. "You tell me how many and I'll tell you how many I've been in." He set the beer down in front of Dodge.

Dodge sipped it and ruminated.

"How many?"

"Lost count."

"If there are fifty different kinds in the world, then I've seen fifty-one." Rudy grinned.

"Ever been in a wine bar?"

"In France." Rudy leaned in close to Dodge to share the experience. "Got to have wine bars in France. It's the national drink."

"They got them here now. In New York. I was in one my last visit. Fancy places, Rudy. Fancy."

"Hard to get an honest drink in them."

"I like wine."

"So do I but it's not what you'd call an honest drink. It's for washing down dinner."

Dodge continued talking about wine, defending it on the one hand, attacking it on the other. It had its place, but it wasn't what someone ordered when they stepped up to the bar. Rudy wasn't listening. He was in France somewhere, remembering something, and there was no way to get him back. When Rudy wanted to talk to you, you listened. When Rudy wanted to think something over, you waited until he came back. You did that or he didn't make you feel welcome.

Westerly was behind them and the train hit the straight that ran for just better than a mile between that point and Kingston. The speed increased noticeably, then began to wane as the stretch was devoured.

"I can set it down on the platform. That's the best I can do." The conductor hefted my suitcase down from the rack with a grunt. "I'm not allowed to carry it."

I smiled my best smile at the pinched-face man before me and hoped I was looking grateful. I'd seen my mother look that way many times, affecting a sort of little girl posture to get what she wanted from a man. I'd seen men do it too, becoming little boys suddenly when they wanted something from a woman, seeking permission, being ever so grateful when they got it. I'd seen Horace do that to Jane and Jane do it to Horace. I didn't like it and I didn't like myself for doing it.

"The platform will be fine, thank you," I said. I followed him to the end of the car and waited as the train crawled the last few hundred feet to the station. I waited impatiently. I strained to see the station house and the cars parked around it. I looked for Dodge's truck. Engine and platform met finally, and the train stopped then jerked forward then stopped again. I moved quickly to the door and waited for it to open.

Dodge stood by his truck, fidgeting, fiddling with the buttons on his jacket, fixing his hair, scratching himself, picking his nose. He coughed and spit and popped a piece of gum into his mouth. It wouldn't do to have beer breath. He tried out a smile and decided he'd better not practice. Let nature take its course. He tried to take measure of what he was feeling and couldn't

Doors slid open and platforms were raised to reveal steps and people descended to join forces with Kingston, Rhode Island. The conductor carried the suitcase to the platform and set it down. A moment later I came to rest next to it. I looked about and saw finally the man standing next to the red pickup truck and smiled nervously at him and waved.

Dodge saw the young woman and started forward. She looked little like the photograph he'd studied so carefully. She was nothing like the little girl at the zoo. He felt his skin prickle and realized he was sweating. He was moving toward her. When he got close he smiled back.

“Hello, Alison.” He extended his hand.

“Hello, Dodge.” I took it and felt his squeeze and we let go.

“Well, you’re here.”

I nodded that I was and Dodge took my suitcase and we started for his truck.

FIVE

Evening came to the island. Gulls swooped and shouted about by the dock across the channel and occasionally by the beach in front of Dodge's house in search of some low-tide treasure. The wind came in off the bay and across the harbor and bathed the island and washed everything and everyone upon it. The animals were at peace. Back in among the trees and bush they were together, families of them, warm and full, content with life, content to watch their young at play and to lick themselves and sigh. I sighed my satisfaction with the moment. I'd been in Middleport for half a day. I was with my father. We were together in his house. I heard a bird sing and another answer. A fish jumped in the channel, and I saw it just as it splashed back to safety. I saw the sails of small boats dotting the harbor and heard laughter from the yacht club across the way. A boat engine backfired somewhere and startled the gulls nearby. A mother on Conway Street called a child home for dinner. I heard the sounds of evening mixed with the silence of it. I looked down from the loft where I'd been for a time and saw shafts of pink and purple light outlined in funnels of magnified dust shooting across the floor of the room. Dodge sat at the kitchen table, his feet bathed in them. I saw him there, immobile, locked in thought.

It had been a long afternoon for both of us. After I unpacked we walked the island. He told me about the house and how he'd fixed it up. He told me a little about the harbor and bay; then we returned to the house and went our separate ways. I came back to the loft and thought about the first few hours of my summer.

The ride from the station had taken place mostly in silence. He asked me about the train and I told him it was fun. He told me about the university as we passed it and about the village of Kingston as we passed through it. We shared a moment of laughter when we got caught behind a tourist who crawled the narrow road that was Route 138 looking at every tree, every blade of grass. Dodge swore at him when he finally got by then apologized to me. When he saw my grin, he laughed and so did I. The silence that followed brought the return of awkwardness.

When we entered Middleport, Dodge seemed to come awake. He became a tour guide. He pointed out Bateman's Lumber and Hardware and the bank and Miner's Shoe Store and the clothing shop and the diner and the library and Sawyer's Market and the drugstore. When we passed over the bridge that was part of Smith Street, Middleport's main thoroughfare, I saw what looked like a very large boy. He turned his face to say hello to someone, and I saw his face and saw that he didn't look quite right. We turned onto Carpenter Street and headed toward the water. I could smell the salt air and I liked it. I liked the old houses and felt suspended for a moment in someone else's place and time. Dodge talked on and on about the houses and the people who lived in them and the people he'd done work for. I heard the names of Nicholson and Armester and Nesbit and Mason. I saw the water at the end of the street, and we turned off to the left before reaching it. We headed down Conway Street, past large houses that faced the harbor and smaller ones that lined the inland side. We reached the parking lot at the end of the street and walked in silence past the Dock Cafe to where the rowboat was tied. It was my first view of the island, and I stared across at it while Dodge lowered my suitcase into the boat. I made my way carefully down the ladder and turned my attention back to what was going to become my home. It seemed a jewel as we started rowing toward it, a palace surrounded by a moat. I felt like a queen about to assume my throne. As we drew closer, I saw the palace transformed into a stone house. When we tied up at the dock I saw a shambles, a place that was falling down, a wreck of a house with junk piled up about it. I said nothing. Another of life's disappointments had reared its head, and I would have to make the best of it. I know Dodge saw my expression. I'm sure he knew what I was thinking. He said nothing and I was heartened. I would get used to this place and he would give me time. I smiled and followed him into the house. I buried altogether my reaction to what I saw and made my way to the loft and fell in love with it.

Now, a few hours later, I watched the gulls, fascinated with the way they soared then suddenly dove for the water, then lifted themselves gracefully to rejoin the group. They appeared to be a group but I didn't know. I knew nothing of gulls. I didn't know if they lived in families or alone. I didn't know if after the young were born they stayed together or went their separate ways. I didn't know if they were intelligent or stupid. I didn't know, I couldn't decide, whether their cry was beautiful or ugly. I listened I heard their wail, their plea, a calling for something that seemed forever beyond their reach and still couldn't make up my mind.

Dodge put a match to the wick of a kerosene lamp and watched the whiff of black smoke disappear into the air around him. He raised the wick some and lowered the glass back into position and moved the lamp to the small table by the foot of the stairs. He lighted another living lamp and put it on the kitchen counter. He poured himself a drink and sat at the table and held the glass in front of him so he could see the light through it. The amber liquid danced. He took a swallow and set it down.

"What are you doing up there?" The sound of his voice after so much silence seemed to startle him. It startled me.

I looked down over the edge of the loft. "Nothing. Watching the seagulls."

"You hungry?"

"Sure."

"I got us steaks." He was looking up, taking measure of me. "Sort of a celebration. You want to help?"

"Sure."

Dodge sipped his drink and thought about dinner. He usually pan fried steak and put the potatoes right in the same skillet while the steak was still cooking. He heaped it on a plate or ate it right from the pan and washed it all down with a couple of beers. He hoped Alison liked steak pan fried. He'd bought milk and soda and orange juice because he didn't know what she liked. When he shopped the day before, he hadn't been sure of anything. He couldn't keep much in the icebox and he couldn't keep it long. That required rowing over to the Dock Cafe every other day to get more ice and that was a pain in the ass. It didn't matter to him. He tended to eat a single thing until he tired of it, then he switched to something else. He ate bologna sandwiches and fried bologna and bologna and eggs until he couldn't stand the sight of bologna anymore. Then he moved on to tuna fish, then to deviled ham, then to the next thing.

I made my way down the stairs carefully, keeping one hand against the wall, trying to sneak up as close to Dodge as I could without getting caught. I watched him fussing at the stove, putting a large old pot filled with water on it, then setting out potatoes on the counter. He was absolutely intent upon his work, and when a board creaked beneath my feet he did nothing more than turn and smile and go back to it without a second look.

"It's not fancy but it'll taste good. I think. I hope. Want to peel some potatoes?"

"I have to go to the bathroom."

"It's outside."

"I know." I stood my ground, trying to call off the urge.

"It's an outhouse."

"I know." I looked at the stove, feigning as much interest as I could in it. "Where are the burners for this thing?"

"Doesn't have any. It's a coal stove. Look inside and you'll see it burning. Be careful."

I used a towel to take the door handle and opened it and gazed at what looked like the boiler of a ship, the kind one saw in old movies about freighters.

"Gives off a lot of heat in winter." He smiled at me, I think enjoying with anticipation the moment of truth about the outhouse. "It's right out back. The only building there. You can't miss it." He smiled again and looked away.

"I know where it is."

"Bang on the side before you go in."

"Why?"

"Company."

"What company?"

"The odd animal or two. Whatever happens to wander in."

"I can't use an outhouse."

"It's all there is."

"I know." I mumbled it. I thought for a moment that I'd cry. It was a terrible feeling and I almost couldn't control it. I didn't like to use toilets that weren't my own. When I was six I'd had to use a bathroom at a gas station and I couldn't. I was forced and I'd gotten sick afterward and had never been able to use a public place comfortably since. Dodge was looking at me, his head cocked slightly to one side, unsure of my problem or what to do about it. "I'm sorry. I can't explain it."

"You don't have to explain anything. But you have to use the outhouse. There's no plumbing here, no electricity, no hot water except what we make on the stove, no telephone, no radio, and no television. I'm sorry. It's the way I live. I tried to explain that in my letter."

I stared at my father for the longest time. I don't know how long we stayed that way or even what was going through my mind. I remember finally only that I turned and started for the door and heard his voice.

"Better take the light. The one by the stairs."

It was just night outside and the outhouse was silhouetted, gray against gray. I moved toward it cautiously, holding the light out as far in front of me as I could, turning about to see as much as I could in as wide a circle as possible. When I got close enough to illuminate the outhouse, I stopped to study it. Surely it would fall over while I was inside. Surely there was a snake in there or a black widow spider. At the very least there was a skunk in there waiting to coat me with that terrible spray. I walked a wide path about the structure and moved finally to the door. I had no choice. My bladder was pressing so hard against my side that I thought I'd burst. I pounded and kicked and yelled and charged in with the light held high. I stood there shivering, trying to decide what to do, when I realized that my eyes were shut. I opened them and was greeted by a bench with a single hole in its middle, a roll of toiler paper on a nail and a stack of old magazines. The smell and look of the place hit me at the same moment that my urgency reached its peak. I took a deep breath and let the door shut behind me.

Dodge slapped the steaks. He enjoyed the sound. They were thin, good for pan frying, well veined with fat. He threw them into the old iron skillet that he'd salted first, anticipating the explosion of meat meeting basic metal, savoring the moment when it happened, savoring even more the sensation of the meat's odor reaching his nose. He poked at the potatoes that were boiling and took one out and began slicing it. It was hot and hard, the way he liked them for frying. He started slicing one after the other, getting them ready to throw in with the steaks when he turned them over. They'd soak up the fat and salt. He was suddenly eager for the meal. He freshened his drink and started setting the table. A fork and knife and plate went at each place. He had no napkins. He was out of paper towels. He rummaged through his closet and found some old handkerchiefs and put two of them by the plates, trying to press the wrinkles out of them with the flat of his hand. He put a glass by Alison's plate, then examined the steaks and turned them over and threw the potatoes in and tasted his drink again. The table needed something. He decided on a candle. There were a half dozen shapes and lengths of them in the cabinet above the sink. The one with the greatest promise of longevity was lighted and held over an old pie tin at an angle so that its drippings would accumulate and become the candle's base. With that accomplished, Dodge set the candle firmly into the soft wax and pressed down until it hardened, until the candle could stand upright on its own.

"I'd like to wash my hands." I stood in the doorway, pleased at my survival, still shaken from the experience of it.

"You okay?" Dodge's expression showed concern.

I tried to nod that I was.

"Close the door. It lets the bugs in. The sink's all there is."

I nodded again and moved to the sink and stared at the long-handled pump at its side.

"Pump the handle. Up and down. It's easy." Dodge tossed the potatoes about while I took the handle and started pumping cautiously.

"It'll take more than that."

I pumped harder and a splash of water spurted out and I let go of the handle and grabbed for the water with both hands. The water wasn't there when my hands arrived. I pumped again, harder and faster, until there was a stream of water pouring forth. Again I leaped forward with my hands, and this time managed at least to get them wet before the water stopped. Dodge laughed at me and I smiled my chagrin and he came to my rescue, pumping while I let the water run over my hands.

"Where's the soap?"

"You want soap too?"

"It doesn't matter."

"Of course it matters. You think I'd eat with someone who didn't wash their hands with soap." He fetched me a bar of rough soap from under the sink and continued pumping until I was done.

We sat across from each other, the candle flickering in our faces, negotiating our food. Dodge twirled a piece of steak in the ketchup on his plate and I winced. I'd been taught that ketchup and steak were like oil and water. He saw my reaction but said nothing. I sipped my milk and cut a small piece of meat and chewed it slowly. We ate in silence, listening to each other's sounds as knives and forks and mouths did their work. I didn't mind. Not as much as I thought I would. It gave me a chance to contemplate the man at the table with me.

Dodge didn't mind the silence at all. He was used to it. The sounds outside his house were enough to entertain him. The animals, the wind, the water, a passing boat, the sounds of life that emanated from the mainland, these were ample to his life. They provided him with what contentment he knew. The presence of his daughter was a distraction that became evident at that moment. He couldn't hear the night sounds. He could only hear the sounds of eating and of his own heart beating in his ears. He was unhappy at the moment. He felt closed in.

"The potatoes are good." I'd been watching him and had seen his expression cloud over and wanted the silence to go away.

"What?"

"I said, the potatoes are good."

"My specialty."

I nodded and stuffed another one in my mouth and the silence came again.

We washed the dishes together. Dodge had told me no, that this was my first day and I could start doing chores tomorrow. But I insisted and he relented and we worked side by side. When we were done he asked me if I knew how to play the piano.

I shook my head. "I know how to play the recorder."

"What do you play on it?"

"*Ode to Joy.*"

"And?"

"That's it."

"That's it?"

"I like that song and I bought a plastic recorder and fooled with it until I knew how to play it. Sort of." I smiled.

"Do you know how to sing?"

"Songs?"

"Songs will do. Come on." He led me to the piano and hit the spot next to him on the bench and I sat and he banged the first four notes of Beethoven's *Fifth Symphony*. "Know the words to that one?"

"Sure." And I sang, "Bum, bum, bum, bum." We both laughed.

"How about *Moonlight Bay*? You know that one?"

"The tune. I can hum it. I don't think I know the words."

He stood and I did the same and he lifted the seat lid and pulled out a handful of sheet music. He found what he wanted and handed it to me. "I've got the sheet music to almost everything." He cracked his knuckles and banged a couple of chords. "Let's try it and see if we get arrested." He banged a couple more chords and we sang:

"Candle light gleaming on the silent shore,
Lonely night, dreaming till we meet once more.
Far apart her heart is yearning, with a sigh
For my returning, with the light of love still
Burning, as in days of yore."

He stopped suddenly and looked at me.

"Why did we sing the second verse first?" I asked.

"I like the second verse."

"I like to begin at the beginning."

"That's a nasty habit," he said. But he relented and we started at the beginning and sang it all the way through, and by the time we reached the chorus, we were belting it out.

"We were sailing along, on Moonlight Bay,
We could hear the voices ringing,
They seemed to say—You have stolen my heart,
Now don't go 'way—As we sang
Love's Old Sweet Song, on Moonlight Bay."

We laughed at each other when done and sang it again and I started yawning. It had been a long day and Dodge insisted that I go to bed. I agreed without argument and after a moment's hesitation in looking at each other, we went our own way – me to the loft, my father to walk along the beach that ran from the dock to the point of the island that faced directly toward the breakwater and the bay. I could see him from my window as he stood there, his back to me. I could see the lighthouse and the light at the opening to the harbor and the lights of the houses that were dotted along the shoreline of Middleport and the tip of Jamestown. It was a clear night, a good night. It had been a good day. We'd managed. My fears, the great accumulation of anxiety that had built up in me over the weeks before I left New York, left me now in a rush, as though I'd suddenly sighed my troubles away in a simple great release of breath. I'd managed the outhouse and the lack of amenities, as my father called them. We'd spent time together and come away intact. Now, as I got ready for bed I saw him and I liked him and I was sure we'd get to know each other as I'd dreamed we would, as a father and child.

SIX

Time creates time. Time creates discordant time and sometimes sweet harmony. Sometimes time, like a great orchestra, can be conducted, and the small sounds and the great, the high notes and the low, all occur when and where they are supposed to. Sometimes time becomes a single sound, a single note repeated over and over. Sometimes time is a mass of notes with no beginnings, with no endings, strings of sounds that cannot be joined. Sometimes time is a song of silence.

Sometimes time hangs suspended like the air on a day that is too hot and too close, a heavy veil that cannot be lifted. Nothing breathes then. Nothing stirs. The movement of timepieces, the rhythm of clocks, the sand of hourglasses, the shadows of sun dials tell lies. There is no time then. The measurements of time are gone. There is no early hour or late. There is no day or night. There is no tomorrow or yesterday. There is only the singularity of existence, of personal recognition, of self-perception, all based on the self-conviction that you are here, that you are alive, that you are in this place, this space. At such moments, that is all you have.

When Dodge was a boy he moved with his family from Boston, Massachusetts, where he was born, to Providence, Rhode Island. He was taken from his friends and the streets he played on and was set down in a place he didn't care for or know. A year later he was moved again, to Hartford, Connecticut. Then he was carted back to Providence. Dodge's father was a promoter, a salesman, a diviner of situations and people. He knew how to take pleasant advantage. He was always on the look for a new line, a new opportunity, the chance to improve himself. It was a lifelong quest.

In Boston it was leather goods. In Providence it was bicycles. In New London it was boats. In Hartford it was food. The second time in Providence it was pianos. The second time in Providence, Dodge's father went to work one morning and never came back. Dodge and his mother and sister moved to East Greenwich, Rhode Island, to live with his mother's brother, who was a merchant, the owner of a prospering dry-goods store. It was close quarters even though the house was large. His mother and sister shared a room, and he shared one with a male cousin four years his junior. His sister moved out when she was seventeen. She was so desperate to be free that she married to do it. The marriage still existed and, so far as Dodge knew, flourished. His sister lived in Oregon, and each year at Christmas she sent him a card with a photograph of her and her husband and children. He'd not responded in many years. Dodge's mother died, of sadness and despair he was convinced, and he went away to college, courtesy of his uncle and the State of Rhode Island. College led to a life of independence. He moved to New York after graduation and went to work for a corporation where security prevailed and anonymity was possible. No one knew of his life before the University of Rhode Island, and that was what he wanted. In time he became professionally and socially acceptable. In time he became desirable. He married and went off to struggle up and down the hills of Korea without ever knowing why and returned to a divorce. He returned to the corporation and was promoted and he married again and Alison was born and he divorced again and moved to his island. It was the end of the story. The generous uncle was dead. There was no family save his distant sister, save his daughter.

Dodge reflected frequently on his life during the days after Alison's arrival. The memories would come, and he'd be stuck with them until they decided to depart. He thought a lot about the company where he'd worked so long and hard. One day they'd called him into the big corner office to tell him how highly he was regarded. He was being groomed. He'd been chosen to move upward. How far up would be dependent on him.

His refusal to be groomed was a signal he couldn't ignore. He hadn't seen it clearly, not right away. When it came to him, it marked the beginning of the end of his career and his second marriage. It marked the end of his fatherhood. It was a slow, indiscernible process for a time, then it struck suddenly. He started thinking about himself, then he became absorbed with himself, and finally he became fixated on himself. He didn't want anything anyone was offering. He discovered that he didn't like himself or what he was doing. Finally one morning he knew he could no longer enter the building where his office was. He would never see the lobby or ride the elevator or say good morning to his secretary or see his office. He would no longer be a husband. He would no longer be a father. He told Jane he was leaving. He was leaving that day, that morning, that hour. He set the terms. She could accept them or not, it wouldn't make any difference. He wanted one suitcase of clothes and a few hundred dollars. The rest was hers. Everything they had. Then he packed and left. And that was the end of the story.

It was the end of the story except that, like time, stories never end. They just are and the people in them just are and the best we're offered is a chance to eavesdrop on an episode. Alison was up in the loft, and she was fifteen and his daughter and the story would go on.

When she was a baby, Dodge had been nearly distracted out of his mind with the happiness his child brought him. She was the center of the universe, his universe, the whole universe. He looked at her for hours when she was an infant. He marveled at her construction, at her parts, at the feel of her and the smell of her. He could never understand, he could never accept that in such an imperfect world this momentary perfection could exist. His depression began when he realized that this perfect being would be tainted, that the process was unavoidable, that he would be part of the process. The pink thing that made those noises, that clutched at his finger, that one day opened its eyes, that one day smiled, that one day walked, that one day talked, was going to end up like him and his wife and all the other people he knew. The thought of it ate away at him until a pain settled in his stomach, a pain that he knew would not go away. When he went away the pain got buried finally, somewhere within, deep, in some dark musty corner.

Dodge wasn't comfortable with time. He tried to escape it but couldn't. He knew he couldn't. A hard day's work sometimes helped. A hard night's drinking created temporary forgetfulness. Sleeping produced occasional escape. Sandy made it bearable part of the time. Being alone, in harmony with his surroundings, being at peace with the moment, helped the most. But Alison's presence nullified it all. Now there were only two places he could be —with her and with himself. And when he was with himself he went within. He couldn't stop it. Time buffeted about in his head during those first few minutes and hours and days of his daughter's arrival. Time dragged him back over the shoals of his life when he went inside, and it produced within him a sorrowing sense of time lost, time never to be retrieved.

Somewhere Dodge knew that he'd lost something of himself, some vital part that he'd misplaced or mislaid or, more tragically, perhaps never had. He hoped that the latter wasn't true. When he dealt with it, he was keenly aware of his desire to be whole again. He'd suppressed that for a long time. Alison's presence caused him to contemplate who he was and what we was doing. It caused him to think increasingly of his father, to speculate about the nature of the man who'd sired him. He started wondering what the man looked like and where he was and what he was doing. Undoubtedly his father was dead, but people lived to be older than he'd be if he wasn't and Dodge dwelled on that possibility. He wondered if he'd ever passed his father on the street or if they'd ridden a bus together. Maybe they'd spoken to each other in some innocent fashion at a restaurant or at a bar. Sometimes, too, Dodge contemplated the prospect of his life if he'd stayed with his family. He tried to imagine himself at the company, a vice-president perhaps, a husband, a father, perhaps of several children. He tried to imagine himself without his island. He couldn't. After several days of such ruminating he decided that he didn't like what was happening. Time was pressing in on him. He was becoming too aware of himself, his place, and his time, and he resented it. He feared it. He began to feel like he had when he ran the first time. He began to blame Alison.

Time played its tricks on the day that followed my first full day with Dodge and on the day after that and on the day after that. In those first days after my arrival I lost my grip on time. I had no sense of it at all. I went with my father to Miss Nicholson's when the old lady passed word through Charley, the postman, that she wanted her kitchen painted. Miss Nicholson put her arm around me within minutes of our meeting and started telling me about Middleport and her family and her childhood. I took as readily to her. I went with Dodge to Singleton's to hear him talk about doing over part of their roof where the weather had finally taken too great a toll. I went with him to Abruzzi's Clam Bar and munched on fried clams while the two men talked about Mr. Abruzzi's new sign. I went with him for a ride in the skiff and we went swimming. We went on a tour of the village's outskirts, through the small hamlets that seemed to me as isolated as Brigadoon. We went to Wickford to see the old four-masted sailing ship that anchored there and to see the old houses. All of it seemed a single moment to me, a series of moments that became one. Middleport's quiet streets and solid houses and people who smiled morning greetings and evening greetings became the expected manner of things.

I met Tommy Raymond, the overgrown boy I'd seen on the bridge when I crossed it for the first time. When he said hello, I stopped and said hello back, and he seemed to explode with happiness. Dodge told me that few people gave him more time than they had to. He told me that Tommy lived alone in a large house his father had left him. He had money, which the bank administered, and he had a housekeeper who cooked for him and looked after his personal needs. Tommy ate out a lot and took the taxi to the movies when he wanted to do that and to stores. But mostly he spent his time on the bridge saying hello to people. His bright round face was alive with curiosity. He'd lived longer than might be expected, and he was susceptible to colds and such and ran always the risk of unexpected death. We stood together at the bridge the day of our first meeting and talked for half an hour, and he made me a member of his gang and taught me the secret grip and I left behind a friend.

I met Auggie Sinclair, the strange old man in the long wool coat. Auggie knew my father's lineage and he knew mine. He yelled it at me from the other side of the street without breaking stride, "Alison Dodge of New York and Middleport, daughter of Al Dodge by way of Providence, Rhode Island, currently residing at Conway's Island." He came and went before I could say anything and left me wondering about him and myself. To be described aloud in such a fashion made me embarrassingly aware of myself. I was labeled.

I met the Armester sisters, the old women who ran the ancient, musty store on Carpenter Street, who sold this and that, and who, I learned, sold mostly nothing. Everything they had could be bought elsewhere for less, and at the same time more important things like food were being purchased. The store would have disappeared long ago if the sisters didn't have a personal reserve of money to keep it going. Their father left it to them, and they saw no better use for it than to keep his store alive. The Armester sisters were an odd pair. At first meeting they seemed more like girls dressed as old women than the pair of nearly seventy-year-olds they were. They had a special place for children, especially girl children, and I was welcome, even though I'd passed beyond that stage, to browse, a practice they generally frowned upon.

And I met Sandy. Sandy had us for dinner on my second night in Middleport. It was a special dinner done up just so. She told me she'd taken the afternoon off to clean up and to cook and set a proper table. She wanted me to like her and didn't mind if I knew that. She was fond of my father and made no attempt to hide that either. Perhaps she thought I could make my father happy. Perhaps she saw in me some sort of ally who would change Dodge and help bring them closer together. It was a good dinner. She served chicken and rice and salad and wine and coffee and ice cream and we talked a lot and laughed a lot. She was pleased with her evening. She was pleased with me. Most of all, I think, she was pleased with Dodge, who was charming and funny and fun.

We sang when we got home that night, a dozen songs, with a passion of people in love with life. We sang *In the Still of the Night*, and *I'm Sitting on Top of the World* and *When You're Smiling* and *Stormy Weather*, and we sang *Moonlight Bay*. We sang until the small hours and talked for a while afterward about Sandy and the evening and we went to bed.

Now it was a week later and it was raining. I became aware of it first as a drumming above my head. The days till then had begun and ended with the sun. The night after Sandy's dinner I'd moved my mattress as close to the dormer window as it would fit to see the stars and the early morning light. I started going to bed early and waking at sunrise and found myself looking forward to it. I liked the time alone at night when I was falling asleep and the time alone in the morning when I realized that I was still alive and would be around for another day. I stretched now in my bed and felt my body within itself and smiled contentment at the satisfaction of it. I propped myself up on an elbow and watched as water met water, as the rain touched the channel in a million places.

"It's raining." I heard Dodge swear it to himself form his bed.

"It's raining out." I yelled down to him and laughed.

"I know."

I heard him leave his bed and shuffle to the window. I heard him yawn.

"What do you want to do today?" It was Sunday and we'd planned a day in the boat, some fishing, some lunch, some swimming.

"Sleep." Dodge shuffled back to his bed and climbed in. "How come you get up so early? I thought kids were lazy."

"I am lazy."

"Then go back to sleep."

"I'm not tired."

The drumming of the rain turned to rifle shots. The wind whipped across the bay and drove the rain against the house. The wind screamed its way through tree branches and wrapped itself about tree trunks and drove the animals on the island as deep into shelter as they could go. I watched the channel become an ocean of white caps and watched and heard waves pounding against the rocks and shore and dock.

"I want to go to the movies." I yelled it above the din.

"I'm not going out today."

"I'm not staying in today."

"Read a book."

"I don't want to read a book." I said it and sighed my discontent. I was unhappy and didn't know why. I had a sense that everything had been accommodation, that civility in the small stone house was a veneer that was peeling away, that had been peeling away since my arrival. I tried to rid myself of the feeling. "Know any jokes?"

"None I can tell you."

I resented his tone of voice. It was snide. I resented his closeness. The rain began to bother me. I toyed with the idea of telling my father a dirty joke, the dirtiest joke I knew. "What would you get," I said instead, "If Babe Ruth married Betty Crocker?" I waited for his response then answered the question myself. "A better batter." He said nothing. "Why do golfers wear two pairs of pants?" I continued. "They might get a hole in one." I went on. "I solved the parking problem in New York. I bought a parked car."

"Henny Youngman," He said.

I came right back with, "Who's on first?"

Silence.

"That's what I'm trying to find out." I tried to do both voices. I worked hard at it.

Silence from below.

"Well, don't change the players around."

Silence.

"I'm not changing nobody."

Silence.

"Abbott and Costello. You're probably too young to remember them. Ever hear of Abbott and Costello?" I was insistent. There was no response. A spasm of sourness swept through me and left. I took a deep breath. I watched a trickle of water inch down the window and watched it join another trickle and watched that until others joined it, until it became a river. I watched as the river grew until it became too fat and broke up and formed another order of things. “Let’s have breakfast at the diner and get the Sunday paper and read the funnies to each other.”

“I’m not going out.”

“I’ll cook breakfast then.”

“Cook breakfast.”

“What do you want?”

“Sleep.”

“To eat?”

“Nothing.”

“You got it.”

I scooped up the last of the scrambled eggs from the skillet and eyed my father, who was still in bed. He watched my every move, feigning disinterest when I looked his way, studying me when he thought I wasn’t looking. “You want toast with your eggs?”

He exploded. “I told you I’m not hungry.”

“It’s going to get cold.” I served it.

“What’s wrong with you?” He wrapped the cotton cover around him as he swung his legs out of bed. I caught a flash of his nakedness and turned away to check the coffee. “I don’t need a mother.” He said.

“I’m not a mother.”

“You’re a pain in the ass.” He stood and let the cover fall loosely so that I’d see more of him, and he took obvious pleasure in my embarrassment. I was riveted, unable to look away this time. He smiled perversely and moved to the table and sat and let the cloth fall where it would.

I sat across from him, looking only at his face, burning with discomfort even at that. I ate greedily, trying to obscure my nervousness. He picked at his food. I started making noises as I ate and he shot me a look of annoyance and it gave me pleasure to see that I'd gotten to him. I smacked my lips and started to talk and kept on making smacking noises as I did, hoping it would make him madder.

"I can make poached eggs even better than scrambled. I don't even need a poacher. Mother showed me how. She's a very good cook, you know." I put the emphasis on Mother and saw that he didn't care for it. "You just put water in a pan and a touch of vinegar and lay the eggs in very carefully. Mother taught me."

I got up from the table satisfied that I'd reached the mark. "You have a raincoat or umbrella or anything?" I started for the door.

"Aren't you going to clean up or don't pains in the ass do that?"

"I cooked, you clean." I left the house.

The rain continued to beat down incessantly against the house and ground, offering no pleasure to anyone inside or to anyone who ventured out. I went into the outhouse without bothering to bang against it. I felt myself becoming saturated with frustration. I didn't want it. I permitted myself to wallow in it.

Dodge cleared the table and left the dishes in the sink and climbed back into bed. He knew it would upset her. He closed his eyes and waited with a growing sense of anticipation.

I returned soaking wet and spit my accumulated wrath at him. "There are no animals in that place. There are never any animals in it. No animal would go in it. It's not fit for an animal. It's disgusting in there, and it says a lot about you and the way you live that you chose not to do anything about it." I went up to the loft and resumed my watching of the rain.

My only complete memory of my father and me together before he left us, was of a weekend together. At least, that was the only memory I felt with any certainty was mine and not something someone told me. Jane had gone off to Boston to see her brother, Ralph, and left us to fend for ourselves. Dodge told me I could do whatever pleased me. The weekend was mine. I could eat what I pleased and stay up as late as I pleased and go where I pleased. I remember going to the zoo. I'd been there before, but always under the dark cloud of adult-imposed conditions. There was a time limit or there were other children or the adults got bored and the visit was short. Not this time. This one time I stayed the day, and my father stayed the day with me. He never tired. He was never bored. We laughed in the monkey house and held our noses and together were entertained by the chimpanzees. We were mesmerized by the orangutans and captivated by the seals and in awe of the tigers and lions. The elephant and rhinoceros were both amazing. The gnu was extraordinary. That's how I remembered it all being on what was the happiest day I ever spent with Dodge. I had as many pony rides as I wanted. We went on the carousel and Dodge got the brass ring. We stood in front of the Delacorte Clock with its beautifully grotesque figures and watched and listened as it changed the hour. We did that at least half a dozen times. We had ice cream and he bought me a balloon and when I lost it he bought me another. We had crackerjacks, and I found, lodged at the bottom in a paper wrapper, a plastic ring with the picture of a clown on it. When I jiggled the ring the clown smiled then frowned, smiled then frowned, smiled then frowned. When we got back to the apartment I took a bath and had cornflakes for dinner and was read a story and slept the sleep of the contented. I don't know why I was able to remember so much of that day then or why I've always been able to remember it in such detail since. I saw clearly the face of a happy man.

Dodge stood at the window, his hands behind his back, the disgruntled captain of a disharmonious ship. He watched the rain and reached with his finger to rub a spot between his nose and eye. He didn't like the rain. That wasn't true. He did like the rain. He didn't like the rain today. It made him feel caged. His daughter was in the loft above, and he didn't like that either. He wrapped his arms across his chest.

Once, when he was younger than Alison was now, he'd gone out into the snow with some older boys. They went a long distance from the neighborhood with their sleds and, Dodge tagged along with the only thing he had, a pair of skis he'd found in the attic. He carried them, with their barrel stave awkwardness, and suffered the abuse from those who were with him for having something so exotic. When they got to the hill each of them used his skis. Then they watched and taunted as he used them and stumbled and fell to the bottom. They left him there, crushed, stunned, frightened. Dodge had never been so cold and angry and unhappy as on that day. He cursed his way up the hill, bruising himself and scraping himself against trees and rocks and the frozen earth beneath the snow. Halfway up he hurled the skis away. He was punished for that when he got home and he was punished for being late and he was punished once more when he fought with the boys who'd laughed at him.

I peered over the edge of the loft and saw Dodge at the window. I heard him breathing his discontent with the world. "Do you think it will rain all day?" I asked.

"How the hell should I know?" He snapped it at me.

"You live here. I thought you could tell by the sky or something."

"I can't see the sky; it's raining."

I played a game of tic-tac-toe on the window, drawing lines through the liquified moisture, making Xs and Os the same way. The game ended in a tie. "Do you have games?" I hollered down.

"Games?"

"Games."

"What kind of games?"

"Any kind of games. Monopoly. Scrabble."

"Are you kidding?"

"Playing cards?"

"Maybe."

"I know how to play gin rummy."

"Will you stop bothering me if we play gin rummy?"

"Sure."

"Then I'll play you some gin rummy."

The cards were old and some of them were bent in ways that, if you wanted to take the trouble, you could memorize and know everything your opponent had. You couldn't shuffle the cards with any sense of satisfaction. There was nothing crisp about them. There was none of that snapping sound that comes when the cards hit each other and fall with a rush into place. They were mushy and sticky to the touch. But there were fifty-two of them and they were all different and they could be used for a game of gin.

I dealt while Dodge finished stoking the fire in the stove. It was damp and the warmth was welcome. He sat down and picked up his cards and frowned.

"You fix these?"

"You'll never know." I grinned and waited and Dodge declined the face-up card and so did I and he took from the pack. I won the first hand. Dodge dealt and he lost again. He dealt again and lost again.

"I don't like cards." He said it as he shuffled for the fourth straight time.

"You'll win this hand." I wanted him to. He didn't.

"I don't want to deal anymore." He threw the cards down.

"Loser deals. That's how it's done. It's the rules. You lost, you deal."

"I'm not going to deal anymore."

"Then I'll deal." I wanted to keep playing and he didn't and there was nothing else I could do. He was bored. I wanted him to scream his boredom. I wanted to scream back at him. I dealt and he won.

"I don't want to play anymore."

"You won. You're on a hot streak. You'll win big."

"I don't want to play."

"Let's make it a penny a point."

"No more."

"Finish what you start."

"No."

"Quitter."

He stayed to play another hand but the game dissolved in apathy. I shuffled the cards and started to deal, and he got up and walked to the window.

"Think it will stop soon?" I knew he wouldn't like the question.

"You asked me that already."

"That was before."

"The answer's still the same."

I slammed the cards down hard. "God, it's boring here." I yelled it.

"Go someplace else."

"It's really boring."

"Go home."

"I was thinking about it."

"Don't think about it. Do it!"

"I will."

"There are trains on Sunday."

"I'll go tomorrow."

"What's wrong with today?"

"You didn't want me to come, did you? You lied when you said it was all right. Why'd you do that? Why didn't you just say no?"

"You didn't have to come. You didn't have to write that insipid letter." He started to mimic me. "I want to get to know you. After all, I am your daughter and you are my father. You came up here to see the freak. To see how the freak lives. Well, now you know. The freak is a filthy piss-assed animal. Go back and tell your mother that I turned out to be a piss-assed animal. Just go back!"

His outburst, the sudden violence of it, frightened me. The silence that followed made it worse. I was still uneasy about my reasons for coming to Middleport. Maybe he was right. Maybe I'd come to prove the worst of what my mother said. Maybe I'd come to rid myself forever of speculation about the man who sired me.

"We tried, " I said. "We tried." I spoke it softly. My voice betrayed my anxiety.

"Sure we tried. We gave it our best." His voice was filled with sarcasm. He turned on me with a fury. "You're a proper young lady from the big city, and I'm an asshole who lives like a pig. Sure we gave it a try."

"I don't think any such thing about you." My anger had become enough to keep the tears from flowing.

"Disgusting is what you called me. An animal. A filthy animal. I am disgusting. No one should have to live like this. Certainly not you. Go back, Alison. Go back now."

I didn't move.

"Go up there and pack your bag and we'll get you to the train."

I protested. "Tomorrow. I'll go tomorrow."

He exploded across the room and grabbed me by the arm and yanked me to my feet. "Now!" He screamed his rage. "I want you out of here now. Get up there and pack and do it fast. Go on." He pushed me toward the stairs and

I nearly fell. I was crying now. I looked at my father and pleaded silently for him to stop. "Pack your stuff right now or I'll throw it out into the rain the way it is. And I'll throw you out with it."

I climbed the stairs as quickly as I could, and Dodge returned to the table. I heard him throw the cards against the wall. "Come on you, get it done." He screamed it up at me. I piled my things into the suitcase as quickly as I could and caught my finger in it when I slammed it shut. I bit my lip until the pain subsided, then dragged the suitcase and myself down the stairs and out the door. I left it open behind me.

Dodge watched his daughter leave and didn't move. He stood by the sink and thought about moving and couldn't get himself to do it. Instead he remembered one of his trips to New York City to visit her. She was ten or eleven then, he couldn't remember which. Jane dropped her off at his hotel and watched from the back of the cab until she was safely through the rain and into the lobby. He took her to his room and dried her off. He gave her her birthday present, a chemistry set. They opened it together and went over the directions and decided that the one thing they could make was invisible ink. All day they wrote each other messages and left notes under people's doors and for the maid and the man from room service. They made a terrible mess by day's end, and they left it all behind them to go for dinner and a movie. The room was clean when they returned, and the sun was shining when they awoke the next morning.

I sat in the boat, the rain pouring down on me and my suitcase, which was still on the dock. My hair was matted against my face, and tiny streams of water ran across my cheeks and dripped from my nose and chin. I stared at the house and waited.

Dodge watched his daughter from the window. She was such a tiny thing, a child still, the small thing he remembered when the world was right. He moved quickly to the dock and picked up her suitcase.

"Tomorrow," he said."

I didn't move.

"Tomorrow, Alison."

Still I didn't move.

"Come back to the house."

I could see him standing on the dock without having to look directly at him. He pleaded with me to come back, to dry off, not to get sick. His face seem lacquered with regret, but I was sure it was guilt that had sent him running to the dock. "Please come back to the house." He yelled it at me. I turned away. "Come in out of the rain." He waited for a sign. When none came he sagged with weariness and carried the suitcase back to the house without me.

I sat in the boat and let the rain beat down on me. I felt the punishment of it upon my skin and the feeling was good. My clothes were soaked through and it was hard to keep my eyes open. I thought I could see him standing at the window watching me, but I wasn't sure. The rain stung but it hid my tears. I would stay in the rain, I thought, forever. I would stay at least until my father came back to me. I wanted him to beg. I wanted him to feel as terrible as I felt. I wanted him to cry.

SEVEN

The day was new. The sky seemed an impenetrable blue. The sun was a reflection of many colors as it formed strings of unconnected glass beads of rainwater in rock crevices and upon the leaves and upon the windows of Dodge's house. The birds drank the fresh water and sang their thanks, and the people getting ready across the way for their Monday made happy sounds of celebration. The oppressive humidity had gone the way of the storm.

Dodge floated in a torpor. He was awake but couldn't move. He was adrift at sea. He'd spent the night on a journey through the dark places of his mind. He hadn't found what he'd been searching for, and now he couldn't move. He felt himself ensnared in a shroud, an enormous cocoon that had wrapped itself around him until he could see only the barest bit of light from outside. Suddenly he was being smothered. It was a violent sensation, and he became convinced that he was going to die. He felt life fleeing his body. He refused to accept it. All the strength he had ever known was mustered and brought to bear against a single point of his surface. He found everything against that spot. He summoned inner resources that were new to him and ripped free. He catapulted to a sitting position. His eyes popped open in terror. He was sweating. He was saturated with fear. He glanced up toward the loft.

Looking out the dormer window, I could see the soft light bathe more and more of Middleport as its source moved higher in the sky. I watched and tried to imagine what was happening in New York just then. What would I be doing if I was with Jane and Horace this instant? What were my friends doing? They were all sleeping. That was what they were doing. No one I knew got up this early. I never had. I hadn't watched the sunrise or smelled the saltwater of gotten close enough to animals in their own places to watch them play until I'd come to Middleport.

I thought about the night before, about coming in from the rain finally, after it occurred to me that Dodge wasn't coming back to the dock a second time. I came into the house and walked past him without a word. I wanted to talk but couldn't, certainly I wouldn't start the conversation. What had happened was awful but the awfulness was mostly gone by the time I walked, dripping water beneath me, up the stairs to my loft. I slept fitfully and woke many times. I saw the clouds breaking up as the storm departed and saw the moon come free of them. I saw a clear night sky, the clearest I had ever seen, when I woke up later. I saw the first light of day, before it was really light at all, when it was still the mere suggestion of a glow from beyond the curve of the earth. I wanted to talk with my father but didn't. I was angry and hurt and afraid.

I pushed against the window and felt its resistance, damp as it was still from the wetness of yesterday, and pushed again until it was halfway open. I could feel the breeze at once, as it bathed my face, as I closed my eyes and breathed deeply of it and let it wash over me. I could smell the coffee below and it smelled good. I was hungry.

Dodge inhaled the coffee while he beat a batter of waffle mix, trying desperately to get the lumps out. He'd searched frantically for the waffle iron that had come in a box of junk he'd bought for five dollars at Pop's a long time ago because there were some tools in it. He found the box and the waffle iron and cleaned it up some and set it to heat on the stove. Now he beat the batter and wondered why the hell Alison hadn't come down yet. She'd been up a long time. He'd heard her. He had something he wanted to say. He should have said it last night. He started for the stairs and saw her coming down and went back to the kitchen. "I'm making breakfast," was all he said.

I used the outhouse and came back and washed, standing close to my father to do so, avoiding eye contact with him, keeping a separate space, staying as near to him as I otherwise could. I sat then and watched him pour batter into the waffle iron and took the cup of coffee he offered and looked away when he sat at the table with me.

"You didn't sleep too well," he finally said. "I heard you moving about."

"I was looking out the window. I'm used to that now. Seeing the sunrise and all."

85

Dodge got up to check if the waffle was done. He was afraid it wasn't going to bake right and tried to calculate on his own when to lift the cover. He stood and waited and pondered. He had driven his daughter from his house. It didn't matter that she'd been difficult. She was a child. As big a pain in the ass as she might have been, it didn't change the fact that she was a child in a strange place with a strange person. He'd cast her out. When she came back to him he'd offered no comfort. Now he would have part of this day with her, then he'd have to take her to the station. He opened the lid of the iron and extracted a golden brown waffle and brought it to her with anticipatory pride. "If you don't want to eat it, you can frame it."

I stared at what he brought as he poured more batter into the iron, closed the lid, and came to sit with me again. He cleared his throat and drummed his fingers on the table. When he spoke he spoke too loudly. He was nervous.

"I read a story once in a magazine about an artist who looked at his breakfast one morning and decided to varnish it. He did and liked it so much it ended up framed and on his wall. It was bacon and eggs, I think. The eggs were sunny side up. I think. It was in the Museum of Modern Art for a while. May still be there. The school of minimal art or something."

I smiled at the story and Dodge smiled back a little and we both looked someplace else. It was a beginning. I forgot about the food in front of me.

"Just try it," he offered. "If you don't like it, you can spit it out. Right on the floor. Won't make any difference.

Not on this floor." He meant it as a joke. I studied the waffle but made no move toward it. "It's probably cold now. You can have the next one."

"Don't!" My voice was harder than I meant it to be.

"I didn't put out the butter. You can't eat a waffle without butter. And syrup. You need syrup." Dodge jumped to his feet and started for the icebox.

"What time is the train?" I heard myself say it, and upon hearing it, dug in. I was putting myself in a position that I didn't like, didn't want. I couldn't understand why I was being so perverse, especially when I was aware of it.

Dodge sighed. "I don't know. I don't know the train schedule."

"Why don't you just take me to the station and I'll wait.

I dug myself in deeper. I sipped my coffee without realizing I was doing it and tasted it and put it down and lifted the cup again.

"Good coffee, isn't it? I make a good coffee."

I nodded. "It's hot."

"That's better than cold."

He started drumming his fingers on the table top again. He sipped his coffee and felt it burn his tongue. He buttered his waffle and he thought about the day ahead. He had to finish Miss Nicholson's kitchen. It needed a second coat. She was a patient woman, but when she wanted something, she looked you in the eye and you did it without even considering an excuse.

"I'm ready whenever you are." I was standing by the table, ready to collect my things.

"Anytime you say is okay." He hesitated. "It would help if you could do a couple things in town first."

I shrugged. "Just so long as I get back today."

Miss Nicholson was waiting for us. She scowled at Dodge and sent him to the kitchen to finish what he'd started the week before. There was a strong note of disapproval in her voice. Clearly people were intended to complete their work within a reasonable time. Clearly Dodge had overstepped those bounds. She was a tiny woman, Miss Nicholson, who stood no more than four feet ten inches off the floor and who weighed no more than ninety pounds. Her hair was a light straw color and appeared nearly translucent when she stood with her back to the light. She wore it short, in a natural way that made it curl just a bit at the edges. Her eyes were large and gray, and they were the first thing you noticed about her. They were like a whisper in a very quiet place, and I kept coming back to them, finding them finally to be warm. She wore a dress and had a small gold pocket watch pinned to it near her left breast. Around her neck was a piece of heavy string that was attached to her glasses. She finished with my father and turned to me and smiled.

We spent the rest of the morning together and I forgot about time. There were sweet cakes and tea and story after story about Middleport and the Nicholson family. We ventured together to farms and distant villages and went off together to sea, making the journey around the Horn to California in search of gold. We traveled on the *Mayflower* and settled in the Bay Colony and moved to Rhode Island with Roger Williams and danced together from generation to generation until we were back in the small room that overlooked Carpenter Street and the church. I hardly breathed during all of it, the old lady put me in so deep a trance. There was such passion in the soft, refined voice; there was such a strong sense of participation that everything seemed real. Miss Nicholson spoke of people past in the present tense. She described them so vividly that I was sure any walk through the village would produce a half dozen of them. The morning passed this way until my father, speckled with white paint, appeared in the doorway. He waited until Miss Nicholson agreed to notice him.

"It's finished. All but the trim. I'll do the trim another time." He waited to be told that his plan was acceptable. She was not disposed to making life that easy. "I'll have to get a semigloss to do the trim," he continued. "I'll get it and finish it tomorrow. The rest of it will dry by then. I can do touching up as well." Miss Nicholson nodded her head ever so slightly and the bargain was sealed.

I called New York from the drugstore to tell my mother I was coming home. As I dialed the number I could see Dodge at the counter ordering coffee. He looked worn. He hadn't said much since breakfast. I couldn't tell if he was happy or unhappy about my leaving. I didn't know how I felt myself. I heard the phone ringing at the other end and I heard Jane pick it up.

"Hello?" The puzzled voice at the other end was expected. Jane always sounded surprised when she picked up the phone, as though no one would really have a reason to call.

"Hello, mother."

Alison, I was worried about you. We haven't heard a word from you all week. I'd expected a call before this. How are you?"

Something about the question rankled me. It was as though she knew the reason for my call. I didn't like it. I intoned a, "Fine, I'm fine, thank you."

"Well, we hoped you were." I detected a note of disappointment. "We're getting ready to leave and I wasn't sure how to get you except to write, and there's no time for that."

"There's no phone on the island."

"I'm aware of that." Disappointment turned into disapproval.

"There's no toilet either."

"No toilet!"

I heard myself giggle and covered the mouthpiece. I had shared something she hadn't. For the first time in my life I'd lived something truly separate from her. I was somewhere she'd never been, with people whom, except for my father, she'd never seen and never would. "There's an outhouse and you have to bang on it before you go in to make sure there are no animals inside."

"Dear God."

"And there's no electricity or running water or television."

"You can't live that way. No human being can."

"My room is a loft and it had a window that looks out over the bay and at night I watch the stars before I go to sleep and in the morning I watch the sunrise."

Jane launched into the litany of sins involved with such a life. The rhythm of it suggested it had been rehearsed, and I heard her voice but not the words. I watched Dodge, who was hunched over his coffee looking very tired, a defeated man, and my heart did a sudden leap at the sight of it. He looked up and saw my reflection in the mirror and knew I'd been watching him. He saw me look away.

"Our flight's not until Friday," Jane was saying. "I'm sure I can get you a ticket." She went on with the list of things that would have to be accomplished in such a short time, assuring me that, though difficult if not impossible, it could be done, that she could do it.

I turned again to look at my father. Sandy had told me that he was a man in need of company, a man in need of someone to care for him, a man who needed someone to care about. She had pointed the conversation at me, but it was clear she was talking about herself. Dodge lived too close to himself. He spent too much time alone. He'd forgotten, if he ever knew, how to be with people. I could hear the sadness in her voice when she spoke about my father. She spoke of him so wistfully.

"I'm fine, Mother, really I am. I just called to say hello and tell you I'm fine and wish you a happy trip."

The final disappointment flooded Jane's voice, and the remainder of the conversation was brief. The goodbyes were mixed with promises to write and Jane's insistence that I go to my uncle in Boston if there was any trouble. I agreed and hung up.

"They're leaving tonight." Dodge was startled by the proximity of my voice. I stood next to him at the counter, and he turned so suddenly that he nearly upset his coffee. "They decided to leave tonight and there's no time."

"I heard you." He swung back to his coffee.

"I'm sorry."

"They're leaving tonight?" He looked at me in the mirror.

"Eight o'clock."

He looked up at the clock. "You'll never make it."

"I'm supposed to go to my uncle's in Boston."

"Ralph?"

I nodded. "Jane said I should call him and make arrangements."

"It's your summer." He sipped his coffee then laughed. "Ralph," he said, as thought it were some sort of disease.

"He's not so bad." I sat down next to him.

"You want something?"

"He's not so bad." I ordered an egg salad sandwich.

"There's a lot I don't know about this world, but one thing I'd stake my life on is that your Uncle Ralph is an ass."

"Please don't talk like that."

"It would please your mother to hear you defending her family like that."

"I'm not defending him."

My sandwich came and I picked at it. "He came to visit us once, him and Aunt Jennifer and their three kids. They stayed a week in the apartment with us. You should have heard Jane. By the time they left she hated them. You couldn't mention Ralph's name to her for a long time afterward. Then she forgot about it and he became her loving little brother again." I worked at the sandwich and Dodge broke off a corner of it and we at it together in silence. The silence was good. It gave us time. He was the one who finally broke it.

"What are you going to do?"

"What choice do I have?"

"There are always choices."

"Uncle Ralph is a choice?"

We walked from the drugstore to the small park at the corner where Smith and Carpenter met and sat on a bench near the World War One monument to the dead. We watched traffic for awhile.

"I'm not going to ask you to stay."

"I'm not asking either."

"I'm not saying you can't stay if you want to."

"What about yesterday? Last night?"

"I have nothing to say about that."

"You ought to have something to say."

"You want me to say I'm sorry?"

"Yes."

"I'm sorry."

"I'm sorry too."

"Okay."

"I want to know why."

"Why?"

"I want to know why it happened."

"I don't know."

"Yes you do."

"You were a pain in the ass yesterday."

"You've never been a pain in the ass?"

Dodge nodded and looked away and smiled when he thought his daughter couldn't see him.

"Maybe I was a pain in the ass, but I didn't do anything that terrible. Not so terrible to make you treat me the way you did. I think you should be honest. If you don't want me to stay you should say so."

"I don't know what I want. Sometimes I like having you here and sometimes I don't. You're hard to get used to."

"You're no bargain."

"I live here. You're the guest."

"I didn't know what to expect when I came here. I didn't expect what I got."

"I told you in the letter—"

"You never told me you were rude and loud and impossible to get along with."

"I am? All that?"

"And more."

"You can leave if you want to. I'll understand if you do."

"I know I can leave."

The traffic moved between the two streets, busy at midday, noisy sometimes as cars attempted the intersection without the aid of supervision.

"How do you feel about me?"

I looked at my father, but he was looking the other way. I wanted to see his face. "I'm afraid of you." He turned. "Sometimes I'm afraid of you. Sometimes I hate you. I hated you last night. Sometimes I like you. And you're my father."

"What's that supposed to mean?"

"Nothing except that you're my father."

"It means something."

"A person ought to know their father. You're the only one I have. It seems simple enough."

"I'm simple all right."

"Well, that's true." I smiled at him and got a small smile back and thought fleetingly of Horace. "When you threw me out in the rain, did you want me to leave?"

"Then I did."

"Now?"

"Now is now. This minute I want you to stay. I don't know about tomorrow."

Tommy Raymond was coming toward us. I wanted to keep talking but knew I wouldn't be able to. Tommy dodged a car and made the last few feet to the curb and jumped up on it and made his way to the park. He shook hands with Dodge and slipped me the secret handshake and winked and said his greeting. "Hi, Dodge. Not working today. Too bad."

Dodge laughed. "Can't work everyday, Tommy. Not good for me."

Tommy laughed his pleasure at being confided in. "I like to work but I don't have to. Not ever. But I'll work with you if you need help."

"If I ever need a man, you're it."

"I'm a good worker. But you have Alison." He turned to me. "You going to work for Dodge?"

"If she shapes up."

"If he pays enough."

"Your father is a good man." Tommy shifted his weight, trying to decide if it was time to get to the point.

He leaned toward Dodge and whispered. "Okay with you if I tell Alison a secret?"

Dodge nodded and slid over to make room and concentrate on the street traffic. Tommy sat in the space, as close to me as he could get, and looked around several times then got to it. "There's a meeting tomorrow. An important meeting."

"What meeting?"

"I can't have a meeting without you. You're number two. I made you number two the other day at the bridge, when I taught you the secret grip. You didn't show that to anyone?"

I shook my head.

"I'm the boss and you're number two. The gang can't meet without number two."

"I'll try. What time is it?"

"When can you be there?"

"Where?"

"The drugstore. The first booth."

I said I'd try and Tommy nodded professionally, trying to mask his happiness. "Tomorrow afternoon. About two o'clock. First booth. The drugstore. The code word is, you say, hello, boss and I say, hello, number two." He jumped to his feet and slipped me the secret grip. "You're the best number two I ever had." Then he darted back across the street to the bridge and took his accustomed position.

"Number two, huh?"

"We've all got to start somewhere."

"You're a funny kid."

"You're a funny man."

I watched Tommy say hello to a woman and her young child. The child said hello back. The mother grabbed him and moved him away as quickly as she could.

"No one pays much attention to Tommy."

"I like him."

"He can be a drag. Once he latches onto you he's hard to shake loose."

"I like him."

"He spends a lot of time in that booth alone."

"Well, he won't anymore. At least not this summer."

Dodge wanted to say more. All he could manage was, "I'll try to make it okay."

"So will I," I said.

We sat awhile longer in the park, then went back to the island. Evening came and we ate a quiet dinner and later took a walk on the beach. We both went to bed early. I heard my father snoring later that night while I looked at the stars. Then I allowed myself the pleasure of sweet sleep.

EIGHT

"You're going to fall off."

"Just pass them up."

"You're going to fall on me."

"Alison!"

"All right, but when you fall on me and I fall off and kill myself, I'm going to say I told you so." I clutched the coffee can of nails to my chest and slowly, very slowly, climbed higher on the ladder. I looked up after I reached somewhere about halfway. "I can't see you."

"You'll most likely have to climb higher to do that."

"Can't you come down?"

"Alison!"

I continued my climb, one agonizing rung after another. I stopped again, and clinging to the ladder with one hand, shoved the can upward with the other. "Here."

"What?"

"The nails."

"Where?"

"Here."

"You'll have to come higher."

"I don't want to."

There were three sharp reports as hammer head hit nail head, then there were three more. Dodge was laying in a row of shingles, the fifth since we'd started that morning. I'd spent the whole time on the ground pulling old nails out of old shingles, salvaging what was decent of both and throwing the rest away. Now he needed more nails. I hadn't counted on that.

"I need the nails now, Alison."

"Come get them."

"Come high enough for me to see your head."

"I climbed another few rungs, just high enough for my eyes to clear the edge of the roof. I could see my father above me, near the peak. He was resting on one side, hammer in hand. He smiled at me. I made a face at him.

"That wasn't so hard, was it?"

"Just take the nails."

"Bring them here."

"I will not." I felt a breeze and wrapped my arm around the side of the ladder and held onto it as tightly as I could.

"Just a few more rungs and you can get your foot on the roof. I have a two-by-four along the edge, by your hand there. Put one foot up on that then the other and you'll be home free."

"Come and get them."

"If we're going to work together, then we're going to have to work together. If you stay there and I stay here, it's not working together."

"Why can't I just pass you stuff?"

"I need help with the shingles."

"I'm still cleaning up the old ones down there." I almost looked.

"We'll do that later. Come on." He beckoned me onward and upward, and I moved my foot to the next rung and tested it. Then I moved the other foot and pulled myself up. I did it again, convinced that I was going to be sick. "Come on." He urged me gently. "It's safe." I took the next step quickly and blindly swung a leg free from the ladder and hesitated in midair and muttered a "Screw it" to myself and thrust my leg the rest of the way to the roof. Dodge laughed and I clenched my teeth and remembered to put the can of nails down on the roof and swung my remaining leg up after it as I pulled my body up with my hands. I found myself straddling the roof's edge. I buried my face against the shingles. "Now what?"

"You have to crawl before you walk."

I rotated myself slowly so that my head pointed toward the peak and, without looking, inched my way upward until I felt my father's hand. I clutched at it and was pulled up next to him. I opened my eyes.

"That was terrific." He was smiling broadly. "Now what about the nails?"

I'd left them back by the ladder, and the realization of that mistake set in with a fury. I was sure I'd throw up this time. "I'm not going back." I said it with absolute conviction.

"You'll have to go back eventually. It's the only way down. The practice will make it easier. Slide down feet first a little at a time. The two-by-four will stop you."

I protested in my shrillest voice. “I’ll fall off. I’ll get to the edge and shoot right off. Is that what you want?”

“I want the nails. Now.”

It was an order, boss to apprentice. I obeyed it.

The sun reached its height and beat down and was soaked up and was enough to make people look up at the sky to question the oppressiveness of it. We worked atop the roof, each on our own row of shingles, each moving slowly and carefully along a twine that marked the evenness of our path. I’d gotten good at the work, driving three nails into each cedar shingle, then moving on to the next then the next then the next. I liked doing it and forgot completely about being so far above the ground. I could even stop for a moment and look out over the bay without the stickiness of fear creeping up on me. The countryside was available to me form the roof, the full sweep of the bay and a good piece of Jamestown and the jut of land that used to be a naval air station. There were several small islands in the bay that I hadn’t noticed before and decided that I wanted to visit. We’d row to them. That morning I saw a speedboat with two kids in it pulling another kid on water skis. The water was calm, almost a sheet of glass, and it reflected the sun and the white sails of boats and the wake of the water-skier as he cleared the breakwater and hit rougher seas. I was watching the water-skier when Dodge saw I was slowing down.

“Get to work.”

I blinked at him.

“A half hour till lunch and a lot to do.”

“I feel like I was born up here.”

"That's because you like it."

"I love it. But my behind hurts."

"That's because you're sitting on it. If you'd keep working it wouldn't get so much use." He grabbed another shingle and so did I and we pounded our way toward the lunch hour.

Lunch was sandwiches, which Dodge had started to make and I had finished, apples, a beer for him and a diet soda for me. We sat under a tree in the yard looking out at the water. "I feel like a swim." I yawned. I was sweaty and my body was beginning to speak to me of the abuse I had visited upon it during the morning. "I'd like to spend the rest of the day up to my neck in water."

"We'll knock off early and go. It'll be high tide then."

"I hurt. All over."

"We'll make it a short lunch. It's easier to get back into the groove that way."

"Not too short." I took a long pull at my can of soda and belched. It made me laugh. It exploded out of me so quickly I had no chance to cover it up.

"You'll get artificial pimples from that crap."

"Beer is better?"

"Beer is a natural drink. Barley, malt, hops, water, what could be bad?"

"The taste."

"An acquired taste."

"And the stomach. I patted my belly."

"What stomach?"

"Your stomach. If you keep drinking beer it will grow and grow until it reaches the ground."

Dodge laughed. He belched.

"My belch was bigger."

"Absolutely not true."

I made myself belch again.

He made himself belch again.

It was a poor attempt on both our parts.

"I'm one of the best belchers in school. But there's this one boy, Pomeroy, who can belch to the '*Blue Danube.*' He hums while he belches. It's amazing."

"It sounds amazing."

"He can also touch his nose with his tongue."

"That's really amazing."

"I can wiggle my ears." He studied me closely while I created the proper facial harmony. I laughed the first time and did it the second.

"Not bad."

"What can you do?"

He thought for a moment then patted his head and rubbed his belly at the same time. "I can also spit real good."

"I know a kid who light farts. I tried it once. Almost burned my behind off."

"I used to moon. Stick my bare behind out the window of the car at someone on the street or in another car. I mooned a policeman once. He was driving home from work. He gave me a hell of a lecture but didn't arrest me or anything. I think he was late for dinner.

We both laughed and were both pleased to have a time of silence to share afterward. It was a good feeling. Dodge sighed and picked up my soda can and looked at it. He started reading.

"This soft drink contains carbonated water, caramel color, phosphoric acid, sodium saccharin, sodium citrate, caffeine, natural flavorings, and citric acid."

"How about a slug of your beer. That's the least you can do after ruining my lunch." He passed me the beer and spilled the contents of the soda can out onto the ground. "You trying to kill the grass?" I tasted the beer. I smacked my lips.

"Thought you didn't like it."

"I just acquired the taste." I took another slug.

"You'll get sleepy. You won't be able to go back to work if you drink any more of it."

"It's just to wash down my sandwich." I took another swig and felt myself getting light-headed. I saw my father smile at me and look back out toward the water.

Dodge was lost. He was in the woods and he was lost. He was eight years old and had been at camp for three days and now he was lost. Early in the morning they'd started an all-day hike. They were supposed to track animals and cook lunch and learn the names of trees and plants, and they were supposed to blaze their trail so they wouldn't get lost. They were also, at all costs, to avoid copperhead snakes. Dodge moved through the woods in a daze, looking up at trees and the sky, trying to reconcile this unfamiliar place with what he knew. Each time he heard a strange noise his head snapped about and now his neck hurt. He was tired, unused to so much walking, and he was frightened and he had to go to the bathroom. He stopped finally and moved a few feet off the trail so no one could see him and unbuttoned his trousers and relieved himself against a tree. He got some of it on his leg and tried to dry himself with leaves and they got wet and his hands got sticky and he wanted to cry. When he got back to the trail he couldn't see anyone. He called out. There was no answer. He ran up the trail and still didn't see anyone and thought he was going in the wrong direction so ran as far and as fast as he could the other way and became convinced that he was right in the first place. But it was too late. He was all alone. He became confused and saw a path, or what he thought was a path, and took it. It let him deeper into the forest, into the bowels of the forest where it was very dark and very damp. He fell. It hurt. He cried. He decided to die there. He found a place at the base of a large tree and lay down and curled up and moved toward a sleep that he wanted to last forever.

"Dodge. Come on, Dodge. Shake it." I pulled at his shoulder and roused him finally, and he looked up at me in confusion. "It's time to get back to work." He stared at me dumbly. "You said a short lunch." He stretched and brought me into focus and got to his feet. "It's a good thing you didn't have too much beer. You might have fallen asleep." I stood and waited.

Dodge contemplated the roof and what was left to do with it. "We'll finish tomorrow." It was an announcement.

"Just like that?"

"Just like that."

"They won't mind?"

"I'm not going to ask them." He started to collect his tools. "When you hire me you get a good job at a fair price. It's understood that I'll do it in my own time in my own way. When that roof is finished it won't leak for a good long time, not the part we've done. Now, what say to that swim you wanted to take?" He started for the ladder.

"Do we have to go up there to get the rest of the things?"

"We do."

"As long as we're there, why don't we finish?"

"That's a nasty idea you're suggesting, work when play is in the offing."

"Shouldn't take more than a couple of hours." We stood next to each other at the base of the ladder looking up at a roof we couldn't see.

"How do you know how long it'll take?"

"I know what we've done and I know how long it took. I know what's left and the rest they taught me in school."

"You're not going to do this all summer, are you?"

"Sure."

"I usually take a week to do a half a week's work."

"That's cheating isn't it?"

"Not if you only charge for half a week."

"You could charge for a whole week if you did a whole week."

"Wouldn't be fun anymore."

"You could double your income."

"I don't want to double my income."

"Everyone wants to double their income."

"I don't like being a disappointment, but that's the way it is."

"You could live better."

"No I couldn't."

"You sure could."

"Young lady, I live exactly the way I want to live. How many people do you know can say that? I work when I want to work, play when I want to play, sleep when I want to sleep, and I am alone when I want to be alone."

"I want to be alone." I mimicked Greta Garbo.

"We'll finish the lousy roof. But it's the last time. Remember you work for me."

"Yes boss. You bet. Whatever you say. You're the boss and I'm the employee. I do the work and you give the orders." I climbed the ladder, shouting at him as I went. "I carry the bricks and you lay it on." I climbed onto the roof and went back to work and so did he.

It had been a good day from the beginning to end. I sat on the dock in front of the house waving at boats as they passed through the channel, yelling, "Evening," at them and getting waved at in return. We'd finished the roof, singing songs through the job until we were done with it. I missed my meeting with Tommy Raymond, but things had gone too well to let it concern me. Across the way I could see people on the terrace of the yacht club drinking and talking and occasionally laughing loud enough for it to carry over the water. The soft thump of stereo music was constant. It was out of place and I didn't want it there. Birds and boats and the water and something of the people who lived here was all that belonged. I looked out in another direction and imagined myself another person in another time, a child in a organdy dress with a parasol, walking primly along a beach, waiting to be called for afternoon tea.

"Soup's on. Come and get it."

My father's words broke the spell. I made my way to the house and the warmth of the kitchen. "Move it," he yelled at me, "I don't want my masterpiece getting cold."

The window was open. The air was wrapped around my body as it so often was at night in my loft. I shuddered a moment of delight and came fully awake. I didn't know the time. I'd gone to bed with full stomach and blistered hands, and a body that ached in protest against movement of any kind. I'd fallen asleep at once. Now I was awake, and though my body was still stiff, I was rested and happy as I looked up at the stars. They were alive, pulsating their life, signaling some messages to me. I traced the patterns of the constellations I knew with my index finger. I found the Little Dipper and then the Big Dipper and remembered their names, Ursa Minor and Ursa Major. The Little Dipper was also called Little Bear. My teachers would be proud of me. I studied Little Bear for a while, then moved what seemed to me a few feet across from the star at the end of the Big Dipper's tail until I found, millions and millions of miles from my finger tip, the constellation Hercules. I found Boötes and Draco and traced their shapes, then settled upon the Big Dipper again. I found the orange star that makes the point of its cup. It seemed to come closer as I stared at it. It seemed to come closer and closer until its brilliance invaded the loft and surrounded me and enveloped me, and for a fleeting moment I thought I understood completely my place in the cosmos.

NINE

I could see the hurt on Tommy's face as I neared the bridge. When I got there, he turned the other way. I stood next to him for a minute, hoping he'd turn around and see the apology on my face. He didn't.

"I'm sorry about yesterday."

"Who cares?"

"I care."

"You didn't come."

"I couldn't."

"I waited."

"I worked with my father."

"You said you'd come."

"I said I'd try."

"You said you'd come."

"I'm sorry."

"You didn't have to work. Dodge always works alone."

"I'm here now."

Someone said hello to Tommy as they passed, and it distracted him momentarily. He found himself looking at me in spite of himself. “You said you’d come.”

“I tried.” I didn’t like the lie. “We got busy on this roofing job. I couldn’t just quit in the middle. Look at my hands.” I held them up and turned them over. He “oohed” his concern for my blisters and raw skin.

“Dodge said they’ll turn into calluses pretty soon.” I heard pride in my voice.

“Girls shouldn’t have calluses.”

“Says who?”

“Girls should be soft.”

“Says who?”

“I don’t know. It’s what you hear all the time.”

“It’s nonsense.”

“We’ll have the meeting now.” He announced it suddenly and matter-of-factly and waited for my objection. When none came he took my hand and started for the drugstore.

The first booth was occupied. A half dozen kids were jammed into it drinking sodas and eating French fries. There were two girls and four boys, and they stopped their conversation when they saw Tommy. One of the girls laughed, and one of the boys whispered something to another and they both laughed. They all seemed amused at the sight of Tommy. They all seemed to know what was going to happen.

“Would you please move to another booth?” Tommy’s earnestness reached my ears but not apparently theirs.

"We're not done yet." It was the fat boy sitting on the outside with one cheek on the bench and the other hanging off into space. His tone was condescending. "Why don't you move to another booth. That one way over there."

"You move. It's important. Please."

"Time for a meeting? Is it a big one, Tommy? A really important one?" The speaker was one of the girls. "We can all come to the meeting. It will be the biggest one you've ever had. Come on, squeeze in." A few inches of space were created across from the fat boy. Tommy stared at it. "Come on," a girl taunted, "We'll all join your club."

"It's a gang." Tommy was red in the face.

"That's even better. I've always wanted to be in a gang." It was the same girl.

"I'll have to talk it over with number two." He looked at me. "If she says it's okay then you can belong."

Six pairs of eyes swing their attention to me. I saw the heads turn and wanted to run. My skin started to prickle. I could feel sweat forming on my lip. My mouth went dry. I tried to smile. I was petrified. The people who were staring were a year or two older than me. They wore jeans and shorts and short-sleeved shirts and appeared normal in every way except that they were suddenly transformed into snout-nosed serfs with dull leers and drooping lower lips and I hated them.

"I'll talk it over with number two and let you know. We'll meet in another booth today, but if you want to belong to my gang you'll have to take orders. Next time I come in I want this booth."

I heard Tommy's voice barking his displeasure as though it were coming from some echo chamber far away. I heard a sarcastic chorus of, "Yes, sir," and "Whatever you say sir," and saw Tommy march across to another booth and turn and signal me to follow. I moved to where he waited and sat where he pointed and tried to disassociate myself from who I was and where I was. I wanted desperately to disappear. I opened my eyes and saw Tommy surveying me.

"You want a Coke?" He didn't wait for an answer. He hurried to the counter and ordered two Cokes and a large French fries and returned. "She'll bring them over." He glanced at the booth with the kids then at me. "What do you think? Do you think we should let them in the gang? I'm not sure. We could use the members, but I'm not sure. We could let them come for one meeting. If they did good they could join. What do you think?"

"I think they stink."

"They're okay. They tease me. I know it. I don't mind."

"I mind."

Tommy smiled at me. "You're number two."

They don't want to belong to your gang. They just want to make fun of you."

"Do you want to belong?" His smile gave way to sudden concern.

"I do belong."

"But do you want to?"

"I want to."

The French fries and Cokes arrived. Tommy shook vinegar on the potatoes.

“What are you doing?”

“Vinegar.

“Vinegar on French fries?” I felt my face screwing up.

“No vinegar?”

“I use ketchup.”

He started to get up. “I’ll get some. I’m sorry.”

“No! Sit down. Let me try them.” I bit into one tenderly and chewed it carefully and swallowed. I ate the rest of it. I took another. “Not bad.”

“We have to make plans.”

“Okay.” I chewed away.

“Short plans and longs plans. There’s a lot going on. We have to be careful.” Tommy bit into a French fry. “You understand?”

“I understand.”

“There are a lot of problems.” He looked troubled. “But everything is okay now. I’ve waited a long time for a number two. Now you’re it.” He beamed.

“Yes, I am. I’m number two.”

“We’ll meet here every day at noon.”

“I can’t, not every day.”

“Once a week.”

“How about we meet as often as we can?”

He thought about that. “Okay. As often as we can. How about tomorrow?” He looked hopeful.

“If we can. If not then the day after. Or whenever.”

“Okay. Tomorrow, or the next day. Or whenever.” He offered his hand and we shook the secret grip. He leaned forward and whispered. “How about them?” He nodded toward the booth with the kids.

"Forget them."

"We'll vote on it. All in favor of letting them in the gang raise their hands." Tommy looked at me so intently I got nervous. "All those in favor of not letting them in the gang raise their hand." I raised my hand and, after a moment's hesitation, so did he. "I'll tell them." And he was on his feet and headed for their booth before I could protest. I left money and tried to slink my way to the door.

"We voted," Tommy announced to the fat boy. "We decided not to let you in the gang. Any of you." He announced it as though it were the most important announcement in the world. He announced it at full voice and spun on his heels and grabbed my arm as he neared the door and pulled me out onto the street. "It was a good meeting," he said. He was all business. "I have to go now." He slipped me the secret grip again. "We'll meet here tomorrow or whenever." He started for the bridge, a preposterous figure, a round little thing, waddling almost, as he took his tiny steps. My heart went out to him.

"Tomorrow," I yelled after him. "Or whenever."

He waved over his shoulder without looking back and I headed in the opposite direction for the clothing store.

I walked the streets of Middleport feeling that I belonged. The shops and people were familiar to me now. A man coming out of the diner waved and I waved back. I'd talked to him once when I was there with Dodge. I looked in through the window of the bank and saw Sarah Haslam frown as she counted out a withdrawal. Sandy had introduced me once when we were walking. I made a leisurely pace, feeling good about the day and the place and myself.

"Hey!"

I looked around and waited as one of the boys from the booth caught up.

He smiled. "I'm Tim." I didn't answer and he shifted his weight from foot to foot. I studied him. He was a few inches taller than me and somewhat older. "Tim Spooner," he continued. "They call me Spoon but I like Tim better. You're new."

I realized he'd extended his conversation to the limit. "You shouldn't treat Tommy like that." I was still angry. "He doesn't hurt anyone."

"Tommy's all right. I like him."

"Why do you make fun of him?"

"We don't really. I mean, we make fun of him but it doesn't matter. It doesn't mean anything is what I mean. We're the only ones who pay any attention to him. He probably likes it."

"I don't think so."

"We don't mean to hurt him."

"It's mean."

"Yeah, you're right. It's means."

"You should stop."

"You're right."

"You should say something to the others. Make them stop."

"You're right. I will. I'll make them stop. You live here now?"

"I'm visiting Dodge."

"You're Dodge's kid. My parents said Dodge had one. You're it."

"I'm it."

"You move here?"

"Just for the summer."

"Summer's okay here. What's it like living on the island?"

"It's all right."

"I'll bet it's fun."

"It's all right."

"I've got a job at Sawyer's for the summer. That's the market. You want to go to the movies with me?"

"I don't know."

"You could ask your father. He knows my old man. He'll say it's all right. Maybe we could go Friday night."

"I'll think about it."

"Sure, I understand. I'll see you." He started away.

"I don't have a phone. How will I tell you if it's all right?" My voice carried the clear ring of interest.

"Come by Sawyer's. I'll be there." He laughed and started running. I watched him for a moment, then remembered where I was supposed to be going and reset my course.

Dodge sprinkled his beer with salt and sipped it and returned his attention to Mr. Abruzzi, who was holding forth on the other side of the counter. He was complaining about the high cost of seafood and how hard it was getting to run a restaurant and sounded, save for his accent, no different than Mr. Bateman complaining about the quality and cost of lumber. Dodge listened patiently as he knew he must. They'd get back to discussing the new sign Mr. Abruzzi wanted after the groundwork had been laid for the negotiation. They both knew Dodge would do the sign and they both knew for about how much. But the ritual of getting there was tradition. It was unavoidable. It was, in fact, a social event and looked forward to by both men. Dodge liked Mr. Abruzzi. He'd learned to be patient with him.

Why then wasn't he patient with Alison? It disturbed him still that he'd treated her as he had. In the days since the incident in the rain they'd done fine, and it seemed they were settling into a routine, but he couldn't ease his unhappiness. She seemed content with things. She was a hard-working kid, a good kid, a generous kid. She was trying to please him, trying as hard as she could to adapt herself to his way of life. The summer was important to her. She'd stayed when almost anyone else would have left. He wanted to meet her in the middle somewhere, to offer an equal measure of himself. But there was a sour spot in him, and it stayed on no matter how hard he tried to squeeze it out. She'll be gone in a couple of months and my life will go on, he thought. I can manage at least to deal with that, he thought. He wanted to, he thought.

"Just a plain sign is all I have in mind. Who needs fancy for a clam bar? Maybe you could just touch up the old one."

Dodge listened to Mr. Abruzzi and took a deep draught of his beer and wiped his mouth on his sleeve and let the taste settle. He saw that Mr. Abruzzi was waiting for an answer. He let the silence settle, letting it work for him another moment. It was his favorite negotiating tool.

Then he said, offhandedly, “You could do that. You could definitely do that and probably save a lot of money.”

Mr. Abruzzi beamed his approval of the notion.

“You could save a lot of money right now and spend a lot more later. You’d need a whole new sign next year, including new wood and fittings and all. And the way the price of everything keeps going up, materials, labor, and all.” He let it dangle.

“That’s a solid piece of wood I have there.”

“It wasn’t much to begin with. It’s starting to go. Touch it up and you’ll be happy for a month maybe. Then every day you’ll go out and look up at it because it will start to bother you that it’s chipping and peeling. Then you won’t want to look at it at all because it will bother you too much. Then you won’t want anyone else to look at it either. Then you’ll have to get a new one, wood, paint, fittings, and all.” Dodge let Mr. Abruzzi absorb the information. “It happens,” he went on finally, “That I have a piece of wood on the island that’s just sitting there doing nothing. I won’t charge you a cent for it. Just for the painting.”

“I want it plain. Something simple.”

“I thought I’d put your name on it.”

“Good.”

“And the fact that this is a clam bar.”

“Everybody already knows it’s a clam bar.”

“How about the people who don’t know? Don’t you want some of them to come by?”

“All right. It will say, Abruzzi’s Clam Bar.”

"Then I thought I'd do a clam on it. A giant clam. An old-fashioned giant clam. Like something out of Jules Vern."

"What for?"

"An enticement. Lure people in off the street."

"What's that going to cost, that giant clam?"

"A lot of clams." Dodge laughed in spite of himself.

"You don't charge me too much for the sign and I won't charge you for the bad joke."

"I'll go home and look at the wood and figure the time and materials and add in the artistic considerations and let you know. When you see the sign you won't care about the cost. That's how much you'll love it."

"That so?"

"That's so."

"Then make the sign and never mind letting me know. Just make it and deliver it. And have another beer before you go." Mr. Abruzzi opened two bottles of beer and insisted that he and Dodge toast the new sign. Then Mr. Abruzzi started carrying on again about how hard it was to run a seafood restaurant and Dodge let his mind wander.

When he was twelve years old, Dodge got locked out of his house. He'd gone to spend the weekend with a schoolmate while his family went off to visit relatives. He didn't like the schoolmate's house or mother or father or, it turned out, the schoolmate. So he left and went home. His own house was empty and locked, as he knew it would be, and he had no way to get it. It was raining and Dodge sat on the porch for a while to avoid getting wet, then circled the place, peering in each window, at first detached, then with a building desire to be inside. He broke a window finally and let himself down into the basement and stumbled his way in the dark to the stairs only to discover that the door to the first floor was locked from the other side. He stumbled back through the dark to the outdoors and broke a window in the kitchen. There was food and warmth and dry clothing inside, and after he had them all he discovered boredom. His solution was the piano. He sat at it and fooled with the keys and became entranced with the sounds.

He inspected his mother's sheet music and tried to imagine what keys he was supposed to hit to make the music sound as it was supposed to. There was a song he could sing and he found the music to it and after a night and a morning of trying he figured out what the notes meant and how to make them sound like *Moonlight Bay.* It brought him a pleasure he'd never experienced before. When his parents returned he was strapped for leaving his schoolmate's house and for lying and for breaking the windows. Then he talked his mother into giving him piano lessons.

"You get something for yourself?" Dodge eyed the package in my lap as we rowed across the channel.

"I got something."

"Tomorrow we can do some fishing and take a lunch and find a new place for a picnic. Maybe one of those islands you keep asking about."

"Don't we have to work tomorrow?"

"Not tomorrow."

"Tomorrow a holiday?"

"All day."

"What's it called?"

"A day off."

"You celebrate it often?"

"Every chance I get."

"That's not much of a contribution to the world."

"I don't ask much in return."

"Don't you want to get ahead?"

"We've had this conversation."

I persisted. I don't know why except perhaps to purge myself of what I'd been led to believe about the world. Everything about where I came from demanded that my father explain himself for turning his back on what everyone else seemed to want. "You should want to get ahead."

"I was ahead. I didn't like it."

I saw that we were drawing close to the dock. "You want to live here for the rest of your life?"

"I like it here."

"Don't you want to amount to anything?"

"Grab that line." Dodge stood as the boat nudged the dock. "Tie us up."

"You usually do that."

"Now you're going to do it."

"I don't know how."

"A couple of half hitches on that post."

"What's a half hitch?"

"Half of a whole hitch."

"Very funny."

"I thought so. If you're going to spend the summer with me you're going to learn about this boat. I'm not going to cart you back and forth every time you want to go somewhere." He showed me how to tie a half hitch and left me there to practice until dinner.

"Tomorrow you'll learn how to row."

"It doesn't look hard."

"It's not. Once you know how."

"What if you want to take the boat and I'm gone somewhere with it?"

"I'll walk."

"Very funny."

"Thank you."

"You want any more of these?" I was at the stove serving myself a second helping of beans.

"Half of whatever there is."

I served him from the pot and brought myself a refill of milk and continued with my dinner. Dodge's concept of food would have made any child in America happy. He thought a menu of hamburgers and hot dogs and spaghetti and steak was varied and healthful and, as a responsible parent, essential to his child. He liked an occasional piece of fish, which I didn't mind. Lunch was sandwiches if we ate at home, cheese or peanut butter and jelly, or more hamburgers and hotdogs if we ate out. It was almost like spending a whole summer at an amusement park eating whatever you wanted. He'd boiled the hot dogs this evening, the first time he'd done it. It was the first time I'd ever eaten hotdogs that way and I told him so and he was suddenly excited.

"You've never been to the ball park?"

"What ball park?"

"Baseball park. Any baseball park."

I shook my head and looked down at my food, trying to figure out what it had to do with ball parks.

"You know who the Red Sox are?"

"Who?"

"I can't believe I have a kid who doesn't know who the Boston Red Sox are. The Yankees. You know who they are?" He said the word Yankees as if it hurt his throat.

"I know about baseball though I'm not too familiar with how it's played. I've never known anyone who was interested enough to tell me. I've never seen a baseball game and I've never heard of the Red Sox."

"Well, you're going to hear about them. This is the year. The big year. We've come this close." He held two fingers together so that they nearly touched. "I remember we came this close in 'forty-eight." He did it again. "This year we're going all the way."

"All the way where?"

"The World Series. You've heard of the World Series?"

I laughed my admission. "I know the Yankees won it two years ago and a few years before that. It's in the newspaper when it happens. And on television. And I have heard of the Red Sox. They're in the paper too."

Dodge could barely contain himself. "I'm going to take you to Fenway. We're going to the first game I can get tickets for. I'm going to take care of it first thing in the morning."

"Do they serve boiled hot dogs at Fenway? Is that what started all this?" I'd finally discovered the key. He grinned at me and muttered something about the best time of my life still being in front of me and went on to describe the Red Sox and the men who played for the team and those who used to play for it. He was happier than I'd seen him all summer, absorbed completely in the telling of the tale, and I was warmed to my toes with the thought that I could, because of innocence of a sport, bring him so much pleasure.

After dinner we took a walk on our small beach. We stopped at the point and sat in silence, looking out at the night lights that marked the entrance to the harbor. The moon was new and the darkness was intense and we couldn't see each other though we were only a few feet apart. We spent an hour there, each of us in our own thoughts, then returned to the house. That's when I gave Dodge the present I'd bought him.

"What's it for?" He held the bag out in front of him with two hands, uncertain what to do next. I didn't answer, and he was forced to deal with its contents. He pulled out the cellophane-wrapped packet inside.

"It's underwear." I announced it as though it were a foreign city whose name I couldn't quite pronounce. I was embarrassed at the giving of it. Buying it had been worse. The salesman at the clothing store had leered, or so it seemed to me, all the while he was describing the various underwear he had for sale and what it cost. He'd described, in unnecessary detail in my view, the advantages and disadvantages of boxer shorts versus briefs and had tried to sell me a box of French bikini briefs, in three colors, for men. I refused that and settled on a package of boxer shorts that were on sale and beat a humiliating retreat. Now my father held the gift up in front of him and looked past it at me.

"For what?"

"To wear."

"I don't wear underwear in the summer."

"To bed."

"What do I need with underwear in bed?"

"I'm not coming down here in the morning anymore to look at your exposed behind."

He was genuinely embarrassed. "Then it's underwear." He threw it on the bed and looked about to change the subject and thanked me. "Do you and Sandy go to bed?" The look on his face was enough for me to almost regret the question.

"That's none of your business." He looked away then moved away, to the kitchen. He fussed with the bean pot, which was still soaking. I watched him for a moment and decided to pursue my interest. "I know you and Sandy make love. I know about those things. It's a thing grown-up people do. I understand that. I don't see any reason to get so upset. I just wanted to discuss it. I'm interested. Not in what you and Sandy do. The subject. I'd like to talk about sex."

"You haven't done it, have you?" He turned to me as he asked it.

"I'm fifteen."

"That's not an answer."

"No." I paused. "Not yet. I just thought we could discuss it sometime. I haven't with Jane, you know. She won't. She can't is closer to the truth. Will you discuss it with me sometime?"

"I don't know. It's time for bed. It's late and we have to get up early."

"Will you?"

"Dammit, Alison, I don't know." He left the house and walked the beach and came back a short while later. I could hear him below. I could hear him rip open the cellophane packet of underwear, and a few moments later I heard the creak of springs as he climbed into bed.

TEN

"Put them in the water and pull as hard as you can."

I did as I was told.

"Together. Pull them together." Dodge yelled his excitement at me, and my hands turned as the oars hit the water and he got soaked. He wiped his face. "Dammit, Alison."

"I agree."

"Let's go back to doing the short strokes."

"I held the oars straight and dipped them slowly into the water so that their sharp edges were perpendicular to it. I gave a short pull. The boat moved forward. He told me to do it again and I did and the boat moved forward some more. I did it half a dozen times without incident and the boat started making way. My confidence was restored. I thrust the handles of the oars as far in front of me as I could and dropped the blades into the water and took a deep breath and pulled with all my might. One of the oars came shooting out of the water so fast that I lost my balance and started off the seat toward the bow. I shrieked and let go of the remaining oar, and Dodge grabbed me just as I was about to hit my head.

"I'm okay." I was angry. I struggled to get upright.

"Maybe I'd better take it." He saved one oar from going in the water and started to take the other.

"Like hell you will." I grabbed them myself and pulled them to my lap and collected my dignity. "It's like chopsticks," I said. "You have to keep them even. When I pull on them they have to be even." I took hold of the handles and prepared myself. "Keep them even and keep a good grip and pull them together." I did all that and it worked. I repeated the instructions aloud and pulled the oars again and did it until I established a rhythm and we moved more or less smartly across the harbor.

"Where are we going?" I'd turned the boat at his instructions and saw that we were headed toward the opening in the breakwater.

"Fishing."

"I know that. Where?"

"Out there."

"Out there?"

He nodded.

"How far out there?" I wanted to know.

"Where the fish are."

"That far?"

"Take it up with the fish."

"It's a long way to row."

"I'll do it for awhile."

I wanted to protest, but my arms and back were tired and the open water looked more than I could handle.

I shipped the oars the way I'd been taught and we changed places and he started moving us steadily toward the bay.

He was lost in himself, rowing harder and harder, absorbed with some aspect of himself that I didn't understand. His face was stretched taut and his teeth were clenched and each time he pulled on the oars a spasm of exertion was evident in it. He increased the pace until the boat was banging loudly against the sea and water began to ship over the side. Water hit his face and he lifted it to the sun as he rowed and it glistened with satisfaction. My father seemed increasingly remote. He seemed to slip in and out of moods, to disappear somewhere deep inside and return only when he was ready. He'd been good company. Our days had passed happily. I felt a growing closeness with him. Still, with it all, I was wary. Perhaps it was his unpredictability. Perhaps in the back of my mind I feared that he might go off at any moment and we'd have another night like the one that nearly drove me away.

He started singing:

"I'll never forget the people I met braving those empty skies.
I remember well as the shadows fell the light of hope in their eyes.
And though I'm far away I still can hear them say, 'Thumbs up!'
For when the dawn comes up there'll be bluebirds over the White Cliffs of Dover."

He studied me. "Do you know the words?

"I don't even know what it is."

"*The White Cliffs of Dover.* Words by Nat Burton. Music by Walter Kent. Came out in 1941 I believe."

"Is that all you know, old songs?"

"Anything before 1945."

"That's rather narrow isn't it?"

"You bet it is. Listen to the chorus." He started singing in his loud, rather flat voice.

"There'll be bluebirds over the White Cliffs of
Dover, Just you wait and see.
There'll be love and laughter and peace ever
after,
Tomorrow when the world is free.
The shepherd will tend his sheep, the valley will
bloom again
And Jimmie will go to sleep in his little room again.
There'll be bluebirds over the White Cliffs of Dover
Tomorrow, just you wait and see."

I applauded and committed myself to learning the words when we got back. We rode in silence for a few moments after that. Our pace was slower now, though the rhythm was constant. "Do you know anything about Dover?" he asked.

"It's on the coast of England."

"It was shelled by the Germans for almost four years during the war." He looked at me with a bemused expression. "The Second World War."

"I've read about it. The people there were very brave."

"It's a beautiful song."

"Yes, it is. It's very beautiful."

"There were a lot of beautiful songs written before 1945."

"How many of them do you know?"

"A few hundred. I'm not sure. We could try to go through them all one night and see."

"You know them all by heart?"

"I do. *Moonlight Bay* is my favorite. Always has been. First thing I learned to play. *Stormy Weather, Cocktails for Two, They Can't Take That Away From Me, There's a Small Hotel, Side By Side, Sentimental Journey*, I like them all. But I like *Moonlight Bay* best."

He turned to look where he was rowing and made an adjustment and turned back to me. "Ed Madden and Percy Wenrich put together a song that almost no one pays proper attention to. All you ever hear is the chorus. The song is music, real music." He cleared his throat and started singing with all the feeling he possessed:

> *"Voices hum, crooning over Moonlight Bay. Banjos strum, tuning while the moon beams play. All alone unknown they find me, memories like these remind me of the girl I left behind me, down on Moonlight Bay."*

We sang the chorus together, me finding enough of the words to enjoy myself, him singing at the top of his lungs, reaching finally for the harmony as he came to the end of it. We finished and passed through the breakwater and the skiff reacted to the rough sea. We were pitched about until Dodge brought us closer to shore. We rowed on until he found the place he was looking for and threw out the grappling hook and it caught bottom and we got to the business of fishing. I watched him bait his hook and stared down into the bait bucket when he slid it over near me.

"You ever bait a hook before?"

I shook my head and watched the tiny fish swimming in the bucket at my feet.

"You've never been fishing have you?"

I shook my head again.

"It's simple. You use a little fish to catch a big fish. The reason it works is because big fish like to eat little fish. And since people like to eat big fish, the cycle of nature is completed."

"I have to stick my hand in there and grab one of those?"

"They're called mummies."

"That's a big help."

"Minnows. You like minnows better?"

I put my hand in the bucket and pulled it out. I did it again and didn't pull it out until my fingers felt water. I did it a third time and didn't pull my hand out until I felt a mummy touch my finger. The fourth time I got a mummy in my hand and let it go and pulled it out and swore at my father. The fifth time I got the mummy out of the water and dropped it back in. The sixth time I dropped the mummy on the floor of the boat. The seventh time I held the mummy with one hand, the hook with the other and with a look at my father that pleaded for mercy, and threw the mummy into the bay.

"A big fish is going to eat it now, hook or no hook." He said it and shook his head and watched me.

I found another mummy in the bucket and brought hook and bait together

He told me to put the hook in toward the back so that the mummy would swim around in the water and appear most attractive. "You're not doing anything wanton, Alison." He was speaking softly. "You're not killing needlessly. We're going to catch some fish. Only what we're going to eat. People have been doing that since there have been people. There's nothing cruel about doing it this way." I closed my eyes and started to push the hook through the mummy's rubbery skin and felt ill.

Just do it."

The command shook me loose from my hesitation, and I sank the hook all the way through. I looked at Dodge wildly, like someone who had just committed his first crime.

"You'll get used to it." He patted my shoulder. "Now, I'm going to cast. Watch how I do it." He lifted his pole so that it went back over his shoulder and flicked his wrist forward, and the line shot out and hit the water fifteen or twenty feet out from the boat. "Your turn."

I duplicated my father's actions and got the pole forward, and the line shot out to the right about five feet.

"Reel it in and try again."

I looked at him helplessly.

"Push the button on the reel, that's the thing the line is wound around, and turn the handle and reel it in."

I did as I was instructed and cast again, trying hard not to notice the wiggling mummy, and got the line out about ten feet.

"That's good enough. Push the button forward and get ready. Keep your eye on the bob. You'll be able to tell when a fish is playing with the bait because it will start moving around, maybe even disappear under water. You'll know when you have a fish. You'll feel it. Don't jerk on the pole when it happens. Just pull back a little. A couple of light pulls. When the fish starts pulling away from you steady, you can start reeling it in. You be as steady as the fish when that happens. Don't panic."

I smiled my understanding of the instructions and hoped like hell that no fish came near my mummy and turned my attention to the bob, the red and white hollow plastic ball that played tag with the wave near the end of my fishing line. We lapsed into silence and did what fisherman do, got lost in ourselves.

Fishing from a skiff on a summer's day becomes a languid occupation. If the fish aren't biting and the water's calm enough you drift off. You forget for large chunks of time where you are and what you're doing and finally who you are. The gentle rocking of the boat becomes your body rhythm and you pass onto the other places.

Trout fishing was the only fishing Dodge's father thought respectable, and he limited his company to people who knew what they were doing. It was not an undertaking for the casual fisherman. The first day of the season was the most important of the year, and there was always a commotion in Dodge's house before it arrived. His father fussed about it for weeks, tying new flies and retying old ones, oiling and cleaning everything, setting out his waders and vest and hat and creel long before he'd need them. Dodge used to watch his father practice casting in the yard, flicking the fragile rod back and forth until the fly came down on target each and every time. His father was very good at every aspect of trout fishing. He was a demanding man in how he went about it. There were rules to be followed, and the relationship between man and fish was best kept in favor of the fish. It was what made catching one worthwhile. Dodge remembered all that as vividly as he remembered anything about his childhood. His father's passion for the beginning of the trout season was contagious. The final twenty-four hours before that day were impossible in the house. The morning of that day began at two, when Dodge's father and everyone else got up. There was an enormous breakfast and hamper of food and thermoses of soup and coffee and dry socks and enough of everything that was required to get through a day of fickle spring weather. When Dodge was six he started pestering his father about taking him with him. The answer was no. It was not until Dodge was ten. That year his father said yes. Dodge didn't sleep a wink that night. The car with the other men would come when it always did, while it was still dark, and the horn would honk three times, and this year he'd go off in it with his father instead of only being able to dream about it.

When the morning came there was a present waiting for Dodge, a smaller version of his father's fly-casting rod and a pair of waders. He was too excited to express anything more than a stammering of his thanks. “Just learn how to use them, boy. Just watch the rest of us and listen. That’s what’s important.” Dodge tried to eat breakfast and couldn’t get it down. The horn honking came and his father headed out the door and his mother grabbed him to tell him one last time to keep his mouth shut and his eyes open. Then she sent her boy out into the world of men. The car ride was wonderful. The men smoked and spoke softly of weather conditions and the places they liked to fish and the accomplishments of the years past. They told fish stories on each other that had them all laughing, including Dodge, who wasn’t sure what was funny and what wasn’t. It didn’t matter. It was still dark when they got where they were going and they had to walk nearly a mile off a dirt road into the woods and Dodge was tired and unhappy about it before they even got to the streams where they fished. He could hear the sound of the water before he could see it and asked, for the fifth or sixth time, how far it was until they got there and got another hard look for an answer. The water, when they got to it, ran over rocks and gushed and swirled about and foamed and, if you knew where to find them, formed sometimes large and sometimes small very still pools. The whole area was overgrown and there was no place to seek comfort. It was a day for fishing on your feet, moving on every twenty minutes or so, working the water to its fullest. There was little talk, and what there was of it tended to be whispered. It was a day of concentration and hard work and the exercise of skills, and after an hour of it Dodge didn’t want anymore. He never said so but his father knew and he was never asked to go trout fishing again.

“What are we fishing for? My question seemed to startle Dodge as much as my own realization that I’d spent the last hour daydreaming.

“Skipjack.”

“What do they look like?”

“Catch one and I’ll show you.”

“Is that all we do all day, sit and wait?”

“You can check your bait if you want to.”

I reeled in my line and saw that half the mummy had been eaten away. I wanted to throw up.

“You been watching your float?”

I thought I had.

“Put another one on and pay attention.”

I managed to get a new mummy on my hook and, after three attempts, get my line out near where it had been before. “I’m not sure I really want to catch any fish.”

“You do if you want dinner.”

“Let’s go out.”

“Can’t afford it.”

“Let’s have hamburgers or hot dogs or something.”

“Can’t afford it.”

“I’m not crazy about fish.”

“You’ll love it.”

“Tastes too fishy.”

“Not the way I cook it.”

My float disappeared suddenly and violently beneath the surface, and the pole was nearly yanked form my hands. I yelled and tried to remember what Dodge had told me and couldn't. I didn't have to. The fish ran the line out some and Dodge told me to start reeling in gently and I did.

"Let him take it. That's it. Now hold him. No, don't reel in. Just hold him. Now reel him in." His voice was gentle and reassuring, and I reeled the line in until I could see flashes of silver swimming and fighting at the side of the boat. Dodge talked to me while I pulled the fish in over the side and looked at me strangely when I questioned the size of it.

"It's too small."

"That's the size they come. Bait up now and get your line back in. Hurry."

First I had to remove the fish presently occupying my hook and did so with much difficulty and with no help because Dodge was busy pulling in a fish of his own. We'd hit a run of skipjack, and by the time they'd moved on we had a dozen of them in our bucket.

"When they're cleaned and filleted they'll be just enough for a small feast. We'll cook them over a fire on the beach. That's how they taste best."

The night was dark enough when we started the fire for its light to lick our faces and make wild dancing shadows against the sand. It reminded me of camp, and I told my father about the place where I'd spent the last five summers of my life. I told him a ghost story I remembered and we talked about Edgar Allan Poe and, for some reason that I no longer remember, James Whistler, the artist. And we cooked the fish. Dodge showed me how to gut and clean them and we did it together and we cooked them in the big iron skillet over the fire and while they crackled we talked about going to see the Red Sox the next Tuesday. Finally we ate the fish. We ate them from the skillet. My father was right.

ELEVEN

Before the Tuesday we went to Fenway Park to see the Red Sox came the Friday I went to the movies with Tim. I'd asked Dodge about it, and he said Tim was okay, but he acted as though he wasn't. My father had the instinct to be a parent but not the experience. His daughter going out with a boy wasn't something he wanted to deal with. As evening came that Friday he could contain himself no longer.

"Where is he taking you?"

"The movies. I told you that. A dozen times."

"What movie?"

"In East Greenwich. Whatever it's called."

"Not a drive-in."

"Maybe a drive-in."

"I don't think a drive-in is such a good idea."

"I've never been to a drive-in so I couldn't tell you."

"It's not such a good idea."

"I don't think it matters. It's just a movie."

"A movie at a drive-in isn't a movie."

"If we go to the drive-in I'll let you know when we get back if it's different."

That was the end of round one. It was not the end of my father playing father.

"How are you getting there?"

"Tim."

"How's Tim getting there?"

"By car."

"Who's driving?"

"He's driving."

"He can't drive. He's not old enough."

"He's seventeen."

"He's too old for you."

"He's a good driver."

"How do you know?"

"His father lets him use his car. He wouldn't if Tim wasn't a good driver."

"Ed Spooner's a nice guy but I'm not sure how smart he is."

"Mr. Spooner said you were first class. That's what Tim told me."

"What time are you coming home?"

When the movie's over."

"What time is that?"

"I'm not sure. But not late. We're going at eight and we'll probably get something on the way home."

"I'm sure you will."

"What's that mean?"

"Nothing. Nothing at all." He looked at me then looked away and started drumming his fingers on the table.

"It's all right, Dodge. I've been on dates before." I wanted to assure him of my ability to go and return safely. I was pleased with his concern and angered by it because he didn't trust me.

It had not been a good day for Dodge. He'd been waking up earlier and earlier mornings because he went to bed earlier. He'd been going to bed sober because he'd cut down on his drinking, and he'd been going to bed tired because he'd been working harder. He liked it and he didn't like it. He felt better than he'd felt in a long time, but it didn't seem to make him happy. It took longer for the days to pass, and he wasn't sure he liked the days enough to keep doing it. He was sure least of all about Alison and the effect she was having on him. She was temporary. She would leave at the end of the summer and he'd be alone again, and he wanted life to go on as it had before she arrived. He'd spent most of the day thinking about his daughter. She was turning brown from the sun and wind. She seemed more in control of herself. She'd adjusted to his way of life and moved now with assurance about the house and island and village. She was graceful in her movements, a young woman more than a child. She was smart. Certainly she could turn a young man speechless. Dodge was convinced that Alison was unaware of this aspect of herself and that made it all the more beguiling. He thought she was probably unaware of the changes that had taken place since her arrival. She'd blossomed in the fresh air and saltwater. This child-woman who didn't wear makeup and who was largely oblivious of herself was beautiful, and it frightened the hell out of him. He didn't want to live with a woman in the house. He didn't want those smells and that noise and the constant presence of civility. It didn't fit. He didn't want it. And the more he didn't want it the heavier it hung about his neck.

"How are you being picked up?"

"At the dock."

"How are you getting to the dock?"

"The boat."

"Who's going to row the boat?"

"I am."

"You're not good enough yet."

"Then you row me."

"What if I don't want to."

"Then I'll row myself."

"What if I need the boat for something?"

"Then you row me."

"How will you get back later?"

"Tim will honk his horn and you'll come get me."

"It will disturb people."

"We won't be that late. And it's Friday. Nobody will be in bed that early on Friday."

"What if I fall asleep and don't hear you."

"I'll spend the night with Tim."

"Very funny."

"Is that it with the questions?"

"Excuse me for being interested."

"I'm glad you're interested."

"I've never been a father before."

"You're doing fine."

"No, I'm not."

"Didn't you ever go out on dates when you were a kid? Nothing's changed I wouldn't think."

"I didn't go on dates when I was fifteen."

"I'll be sixteen soon."

"Not when I was sixteen either."

"What did you do when you were fifteen?"

Dodge thought about the question. When he was fifteen he lived in Providence. They were living in a large house and they were living well. Fifteen was when his father went to work one morning and didn't come back. "Nothing," he said. "When I was fifteen I did nothing."

"You went to school."

"Yes, I went to school. I was in my second year of high school. We lived in Providence. Then we moved."

"Why?"

"We moved. That's all."

"Did you have any friends?"

"I knew kids. No real friends. We moved too much for that. I don't really want to talk about it."

"What kind of kid were you?"

"What time is Tim coming?" He asked it gruffly.

"Soon. You really never had any dates when you were fifteen?"

"I most likely had a few."

"Why are boys so nervous around girls?"

"Nervous?"

"A lot of boys sweat when they talk to girls. Did you stammer and sweat?"

"Sometimes. I don't much anymore. There's not much to sweat about anymore. Don't you have to do something to get ready?"

"Did you ever have fun when you were a kid?"

"I've had fun my whole life, until now, until all these questions."

I kissed my father on the cheek and laughed and ran up to the loft. I hummed my happiness while I got changed. I felt good. I was happy. I could hear Dodge moving about below, snorting a complaint about something. "What are you doing tonight?"

"What I usually do, nothing."

"Want to come with us?"

"I'd only look crazy."

"Maybe sometime you and Sandy and me and whoever could double-date."

"Fat chance."

"Will you be lonely alone?"

"I'm too fond of my own company to get lonely."

"You should live in a lighthouse."

"If you don't stop bugging me I'm going to."

A horn honked across the channel, and I could see Tim getting out of his car. He walked to the dock and sat on one of the pilings.

"I need your help." Dodge looked up at me from the can of beans he was eating. "You have to zip me." I smiled at his expression of concern. "My zipper. I can't get it up without help. Get a can opener." He stared dumbly at me. "I'm going to be late."

Dodge fetched a beer can opener and waiting for further instructions. He had no idea what I was talking about.

"I'll hold the top of my pants together and you use the point on the can opener to pull the zipper up." He stood, immobilized. "Come on, Dodge, help me."

Dodge stuck the point of the can opener in the hole of the zipper and pulled on it. Nothing happened. "They're too tight. You can't wear pants that tight. Your whatsis sticks out too far. Your ass."

"They're not too tight."

"If they're not too tight how come you have to have someone close the zipper with a can opener?"

"The zipper is too tight."

"Move your hand." He barked the command and took hold of the top of my pants and pulled up on them and the zipper and the same time and got the zipper halfway up. "Does it take a can opener to get them off?"

"No." I laughed.

"Too bad."

"But it takes a can opener to get them back on again."

Dodge grunted his approval and got the zipper the rest of the way up and stood back to see if his daughter was going to explode from the pressure. He watched as she bent her knees once and touched her toes and smiled her thanks.

"Are you going to row me?"

Dodge nodded and we left the house. I entered the warm evening air and breathed deeply of it. I could see Tim and I waved to him and he waved back. I saw my father scowl. We rowed the channel in silence. When I started to climb the ladder to Tim, Dodge grunted and I turned to look down at him. “I’ll be all right,” I said.

He pushed the boat away and started rowing back to the island. I watched him from the top of the ladder. He looked lonely.

It was dark when he got back to the house. He lighted a lamp and poured himself a tumbler of whiskey and sat down to contemplate himself. He felt like doing that. He wanted to lay it all out where he could abuse it. He wanted to feel as bad as he could possibly feel. He studied the oil lamp in front of him and laughed at it. He was a man living in the last half of the twentieth century who chose to live as a man in the century past. He knew that about himself. He knew he’d have been happier in another time, a simpler time, perhaps as a ship’s officer. He wouldn’t have wanted to be captain. He was sure responsibility would sit no better on him than it did now. Second mate, third mate, that’s what he had in mind for himself. To live a little better than the crew but not so much better that pressure was put upon him because of it. Then he realized what he was thinking was absurd. He was alive now, living as he chose to live. Auggie Sinclair and Tommy Raymond and Miss Nicholson, they all lived as they chose to, given the circumstances of their lives. They made the best of it, turning what they had and who they were into their own peculiar definition of life. That’s all he was doing. He was living alone on an island in a world in which there were no longer islands. He’d run. He’d escaped. He’d freed himself, he thought, from the hollow life of the twentieth century man. But he hadn’t run anywhere. He was isolated on his island, but it was in his mind where isolation mattered. He was living exactly as he wanted to live. He told himself so. He told himself constantly. He told himself that so often he wondered if he wasn't conning himself into believing he'd achieved something when all he'd really done was allow himself to wallow in his own eccentricity. He poured himself another drink and stared at the lamp and felt himself drifting. He felt himself being mesmerized by the flickering light and its shadows. He knew he had control of himself. He could speak if he wanted to. He could scream. He could move his fingers and arms and legs and eyes. He could stand and move away from the table. He could break the trance. But he didn't. He wanted it this way and he allowed it to happen. Or perhaps he made it happen. He tried to determine which of these was the case and lost track of himself before he ever knew. He didn't care. He saw himself sitting at the table. He stood in the corner and saw himself at the table, a magnified vision like a fish in a curved bowl. The man he saw was a familiar stranger. He recognized the face and figure. He saw a man of fifty who needed a shave and a bath and a haircut. He moved closer to study the man better. He saw weariness in the man's face. He saw fear. Was that possible? Fear? Why would such a man be afraid? What was there in this life to cause the lines of fear to become etched upon the skin? He watched the man swallow the drink before him and saw him pour another. There was misery in the man. It was apparent that there was a place inside the man that had turned against him, a traitor of the spirit that lay buried beneath other emotions and ate away at the man's life.

I didn't know what my father was thinking and feeling while I was at the movies. There was no reason for me to know, no way I could or should have known what was at the root of the man. I was preoccupied with my delight at the experience of a drive-in movie theatre. The Volkswagen bus in front of us was rocking with such violence that I was certain it would explode. I looked inside on my way to the snack bar and saw a man and a woman and at least half a dozen kids. Their speaker was turned all the way up and it still wasn't loud enough to drown out the yelling, and even with all that everyone had their eyes glued to the screen. There was a couple in the car next to us, and they were kissing passionately, their faces moving in slow circles, their jaws working up and down. The girl opened her eyes once and looked directly at me while the boy kissed her. She returned the kiss and kept her eyes open and locked with mine. It frightened me. What was in that stare? How could you give yourself to an embrace and exchange so passionate a kiss and look, without feeling, at an intruder. Was it obedience to expectation? You dated. You kissed. You explored. You did these things, performed the rituals, whether feeling accompanied them or not? I hoped such was not the case. I wanted desperately to believe that feelings were essential to such intimacy. Tim's hand moved to my shoulder and I looked over at him and smiled. He smiled back and returned his attention to the film.

Tim was the first boy I'd ever gone on a date with in a car. I wondered about that, about the lack of supervision, about the absence of anyone who could look with disapproval in the mirror, who could clear their throat. I'd been alone with boys before, but there was always someone in the next room or someone expected home momentarily. I wondered if Tim would kiss me. I wanted him to. I wondered if he'd try more. I wasn't at all sure about that. I thought about it a great deal. I thought about having sex, about when I'd have it for the first time and who I'd have it with and what it would be like. I didn't know the answers to any of my questions. You couldn't plan things like that, not altogether. I watched Tim and moved a little closer to him. His hand closed over my shoulder and I snuggled up next to him. His body warmth was nice. He was nice. He was a good person, I was sure of that. He was a person of substance, a person who would stand by you, a person who wouldn't use you. He was a person, the kind of person, I'd thought about having my first sexual experience with. It would be better to have it here than in New York, better to have it far away from Jane, better to have it with someone I wouldn't have to see every day for the next few years, until I left high school and went away to college. I wondered how Tim felt about it. I wondered if he'd ever had sex before. I wondered if he wanted to have sex with me.

"You like Middleport?" Tim's voice shook me loose from my thoughts. I nodded that I did and dipped into the bucket for more popcorn and kept my eyes on the screen. I was afraid, I think, that he'd be able to read my mind if he saw my face.

"It's okay," he continued, "but I'm not going to stay. I'm going to the state college, URI. It's all we can afford. When I graduate from there I'm getting out. What's it like in New York? I might go there."

"It's okay."

"It has to be better than okay." He protested and turned his attention completely away from the film. "I don't know what I'm going to do yet but I'm going to do it there." He seemed to decide on the spot.

"I guess I don't pay much attention to it. I've lived there all my life. It's like you living here."

"How do you like living on the island with Dodge?"

"It's different."

"It must be. He's strange, your father. Some of the kids think he's crazy." He tried immediately to temper what had obviously upset me. "I don't think so. It's just that he lives alone over there and he doesn't talk much to people."

"He likes his privacy."

"My mother says he's trying to forget something that made him very unhappy. My father says he's a good man who minds his own business and that the world would be better off if there were more of him."

"He lives the way he wants to live." There was an edge to my voice and I liked it. I liked defending him.

"I like your father." The expression on Tim's face was so pained I wanted to laugh. He had started what he thought would be an interesting conversation and ended up getting himself into trouble.

"I like him too." I smiled.

"I'm sorry."

"There's nothing to be sorry about."

"I don't want you to be mad at me."

"I'm not mad at you." I kissed him quickly and it suddenly became passionate. We kissed for the longest time and parted finally and I felt off balance. I wanted to do it again.

"What are you going to do the rest of the summer?"

"Work with my father. He's been teaching me to use his tools, to do carpentry and to paint. Stuff like that."

"You like it?"

"I love it."

"How old are you?"

"Almost sixteen."

"I'm just seventeen."

An explosion on screen interrupted us. A house shattered into a million bits. We watched as the roof fell to the ground, crushing everything beneath it, everything but the grade B James Bond character who emerged unscathed and who gave chase after the villains in his sports car.

"What grade are you in?"

"Tenth. Second form we call it. I go to a private school."

"I'm in eleventh," he said.

On the screen, a helicopter swooped down and snatched up the villain, then turned and started to chase the hero. It dropped a bomb on him. The hero pushed a button that caused the roof of his car to stretch as tight as a trampoline, and the bomb hit it and bounced off and hit the helicopter and it disappeared in flame and smoke.

"You like the movie?"

"I think it's funny." We smiled out mutual lack of regard for the film and kissed again.

"You want to go somewhere?"

My expression conveyed my concern at the question and he saw it at once. He was as nervous as I was, maybe more so.

"We could get a hamburger or something."

I continued to stare.

"A lot of kids will be there."

I nodded and we removed the speaker from his window and slowly left the place, making as little noise as possible, not turning on our lights until we'd reached the small back road that led to the highway. As we left I watched the screen and saw the villain parachute from the wreckage of the helicopter into a speeding boat that was pulling a man on water skis —the hero.

Dodge merged with himself and became conscious of his presence at the table. He didn't want to be there. He didn't want to deal with his feelings. He had never liked dealing with them. Repress what you feel. He'd done that since he was a boy. His father, to whom he wanted to be close, had never revealed anything of himself. When his father left Dodge turned to his mother, but she had her own difficulties. They moved to live with her brother, and she spent the rest of her life trying not to be ashamed of herself for having to do it. He felt somehow responsible for his mother's unhappiness and, though no one ever said it was so, the feeling grew over the years. His mother relied on him for emotional support and he didn't like that either. He rejected the role and turned inward, and when he discovered no comfort there, he tried to reject all feeling. Feeling was a waste of time and effort and resulted only in pain. He felt, or supposed he felt, nothing for his mother or sister or himself. He felt nothing for anyone, not the girls he dated, not the people he spent time with in school. He spent increasing amounts of time alone and became suspect because of it.

After they lived with his uncle for a time, Dodge was called down to his store. His uncle wanted to have a man-to-man talk with him. His uncle wanted to set out the realities of life and did so, much as one deals playing cards out on the table. He dealt them all face up because he was honest and because it never occurred to him that a young man didn't need to know them all, not all at once. His uncle spoke from experience. His uncle, who was a ruddy man with large ears, judged everything by what he knew of it firsthand and thus had no insight into his own children much less Dodge. It did not occur to the man that anyone should behave differently in this world than he did.

"You're a good boy, Albert," he said after staring at Dodge for the length of time calculated to make him uncomfortable. "You're a good boy. You do your chores and you're respectful of your elders. I like that about you. I wouldn't be taking the time to talk to you if I didn't think you were worth it."

Dodge shifted his weight and waited. He was seated in a large wooden chair across from his uncle's massive desk trying to look impressed and interested.

"I have in mind," his uncle went on, "you working in the store this summer and next, until you're ready for college. When the time for that comes, I'll send you to the state college. I'll pay you for working here and I'll pay the cost of your education. I'll do that for your mother and for you. You're a good boy. You deserve more than what your father gave you."

Dodge bristled at the mention of his father. His uncle saw it. "You're old enough to face the truth. Your father was irresponsible. He never held a regular job. He never owned a house." He saw Dodge flinch. "All those places were rented. The reason you kept moving was because he couldn't make rent. He got into debt and moved to a place where he wasn't known. He was a bum. He spent on himself then gave what was left over, if there was anything, to your mother. It was a blessing when he deserted you. At least now your mother is being looked after and you'll have a proper education."

Dodge had protested this characterization of his father, and his uncle let him do it for a while. Then slammed his fat fist down on the desk top.

"You don't know what you're talking about, boy. One day you'll understand. If you don't like the truth right now, put it aside for awhile. You'll come back to it one day."

Dodge stood to leave. His uncle wouldn't let him. "I have another thing to say. It's about your mother. She's not had a happy life. I want you to think about her more and spend more time with her." Dodge started to say something but his uncle put up a hand. "I know you think you do right by her but you don't. A woman needs attention. She needs it from someone she loves. She doesn't love me, Albert. I'm connected with her unhappiness in this world and I always will be. She loves you. You're all she's got to bring her joy." He paused and riveted his small black eyes on Dodge. "Your mother needs you and I want you to be more mindful of her."

"Yes, sir." Dodge's response is what his uncle wanted, and he smiled and got up from behind his desk and came around it and put his hand on his nephew's shoulder. "I know you'll do what's expected. You've got blood from my side of the family. It's good blood." His uncle fished into his pocket and drew out a clump of paper money. "It's a month yet before summer and you can earn anything." He separated a five-dollar bill from the clump and put the rest away. "Take this and use it on what you want. A young man should have some money for that purpose."

The recollection of that year came to Dodge because his daughter had asked him what life was like when he was fifteen. The bottle in front of him was half gone. The lamplight cut across his glass of liquor, and he could see his distorted image in it. He hadn't liked being fifteen. He hadn't liked any of his time after his father left, and college became his path of escape. He dreamed of it and spent more time with his mother and drew farther away from her as a consequence. He and his sister shared an unspoken commitment to finding another life as soon as possible. When he finally managed it, he began feeling guilty. From a distance his mother became a figure who made him cry. She was a good person, a woman whose life had been disappointment heaped upon disappointment, who, if she ever had dreams, abandoned them long ago in return for a marginal handhold on emotional survival.

His mother and uncle were long dead, leaving him with memories that confused and angered him. They brought him no peace.

Dodge thought of his marriages, of his attempts to have a relationship with another person, of the deep disappointment he'd suffered each time. It was true that he'd caused more pain than he suffered and he regretted that. He regretted a great deal. He wondered often what would have happened if he'd tried harder, if some aspect of his life had gone differently. He looked about the room and wondered. He poured himself another drink, and it splashed on him when he raised his glass to drink it. He wiped his mouth and grinned at himself foolishly. He thought about Alison. Had she come to test him? Was she just another in the line of people who wanted something from him, something that he didn't have to give? Was all that he felt now for his daughter going to blow up in their faces as it had with her mother? Why had she come? To what end? To spite her mother? He knew Alison's mother hated him. Probably with cause. She wasn't a bad person, Alison's mother, just one of those who equated life with material possessions. From morning till night her mind was occupied only with her place in life and what was required to maintain it with stability. She loved her child. Dodge knew that. He knew that once she had probably loved him. The problem had been within him more than her. She'd always been consistent, he could say that for her. She was the same in marriage as before it. He hated not being able to respond to someone. He hated himself for not being able to offer something to either of the women who'd married him or to Alison. He despised himself for it. He poured what was left of his drink down his throat and stood and lurched to one side and caught himself by holding on to the table. He was drunk, good and drunk. He looked up toward the loft. Who the hell did she think she was coming up here to do this to him? What right had she to cause him all this pain? He'd fix her like he fixed the others who had tried to get something from him. He'd make her regret even the trying of it. He started for the stairs.

The car was parked near the dock. Its lights were out. I sat next to Tim in silence, looking across at the darkness of the island. We sat, two children with adult yearnings, wanting to deal with them but uncertain, unable to decide whether to proceed. I felt little bumps on my body and shivers running around inside. I felt fuzzy. I felt like I'd never felt in my life. I looked at Tim and wondered what he was feeling. I wanted him to know how I felt. I wanted him to feel the same way.

"I'm glad you asked me to the movies."

Tim had been waiting for a gracious way to say goodnight. He, too, was experiencing confusion. Some of his feelings were the same as Alison's, some were his own, born of frustration and misunderstanding. He thought she'd had a bad time and that maybe she was too young and that there was probably no chance they'd go out again. "It wasn't a very good film," he said.

"It doesn't matter."

"It was kind of funny though when the bad guy got shot off into space accidentally."

"It was kind of stupid."

We lapsed into silence again. Our hands were next to each other's on the seat. I took his and held it. "I guess you'd better honk the horn."

"Oh, yeah. Right." Tim honked three times then looked over at me for approval. We were still holding hands.

"It'll take him a few minutes to row over." I squeezed his hand and we looked at each other and we kissed. We kissed a long time.

"Will you go out with me again?"

"I'd like to. A lot."

"I can get the car next week. We could go to the movies or out with some of the kids or just go somewhere to talk and be alone."

"I'd like that."

"Do you ever go to the beach?"

"Sure."

"We could do that too. I can get an afternoon off and we can do that."

"It's a deal."

We kissed again.

"Are you working tomorrow?"

"Yeah. Saturday is a big day."

"I'll come by the store if I can."

"Good. Come by. I get a half hour for lunch. I usually eat out back but we could go for a walk."

"I'll try. But don't worry if I don't make it. Dodge might want to work."

"I won't worry. You'll try to come?"

Dodge's lantern could be seen in the bow of the boat as he rowed slowly across the channel. I got out of the car and Tim started to follow. "You go on. It's better. I'll see you tomorrow if I can." We kissed once more and Tim started the car and drove off slowly as I walked to the dock and waited. I watched the boat as it got closer and could see the back of my father's head as he reached the far end of the dock. I climbed down the ladder slowly and moved to the stern of the boat and sat. He pushed off and turned the boat back toward the island, and I saw his face in the light for just a moment before we passed back into the darkness of the night. It was the face of a demon. I stifled a scream and he saw me do it and leered.

"Did you have a good time at the movies?" His voice was slurred and he slipped in his seat.

"Yes, I did, thank you." My reply was formal, but the fear in me was betrayed by the quivering of my voice.

"I'll bet you did. I had a good time too."

"You look it."

He giggled. "I had a good time too." He said it to himself the second time and pushed on, rowing sloppily, working against the tide, banging into the dock when we reached it. I got out of the boat as quickly as I could and ran to the house. I could hear Dodge stumbling out of the boat and laughing.

The loft was havoc. My clothes had been thrown about from one end of it to the other. My bed was jammed into the corner and the sheets on it had been ripped to shreds. My personal things were scattered about. Nothing had been spared the violence and cruelty of his attack. I heard him come in. He moved to the piano and began playing, *Moonlight Bay*. I ran down the stairs and saw him turn toward me and smile. He giggled. I moved toward him as if on a track. I raised my hand and brought it down on his face with all my might. The sound of flesh hitting flesh echoed like a rifle report. He kept playing. I hit him again. He kept playing.

"I could feel the tears running across my cheeks. I felt the rage in me as a pressure that was going to become too great and explode and destroy me. He rocked back and forth on the piano stool and kept playing. I kept hitting him, and he absorbed each blow as though he wanted it. "I hate you. You left me. You left me alone. You didn't ask me. You didn't care. You left me and I hate you." I heard my screams but didn't recognize them as my own. It was a dark voice, low and raspy, a voice that spoke now without any help from me. "Do you know what it's like to be five years old and have your father walk out one day and never come back, never say why, never say anything?" I hit him again and he kept playing. "I want to kill you. I've always wanted to kill you." I hit him again. "I wish I knew how to kill you. I wish I could kill you for every night I've cried and didn't know why. I wish I could kill you for not liking my mother better, for not having feelings, for making me blame myself for your leaving." I hit my father again and again and again until I was too weary to hit him anymore.

He seemed cemented to the place where he sat. He weaved back and forth in front of me and looked at me without changing expression. I left him that way, moving to the door, leaving it open behind me, leaving him, I hoped, to die.

Dodge stared at the open door, conscious of an urge to cry out, to call his daughter back, but there was no sound within him. He felt himself slipping toward unconsciousness. It felt as if he were falling asleep. He didn't want to sleep. He was afraid he wouldn't wake up. Often in his life he'd wanted to die but not now. He experienced urgency, a sensation that flooded his body, an overwhelming desire to live. Then he let himself down to the floor.

I untied the boat and stepped into it and took the oars that he'd left in the locks and began rowing. I did not have the lamp nor any of my things. It hadn't occurred to me and didn't as I pulled out into the channel to bring anything. I didn't row toward the dock on the other side. I don't know why I didn't. I moved instead toward the open harbor. I tried to remember what I knew of rowing and concentrated on that and gave no thought at all to my destination. I worked at establishing a steady pace and felt some progress in doing that and looked over my shoulder finally to see where I was. I cleared the channel and moved out into wider water. I moved quickly and realized that the tide was going out and was taking me with it, that the water was rough and that it was windy. I was frightened then and fought to control my destiny but could not. I thought to use the tide to my advantage and move toward some point of land, perhaps the town dock or marina where I would be safe. But there was no way I could calculate such a thing and no way I could fight the tide, and I found myself heading resolutely toward the breakwater and the bay. I could hear the bell clanging its lament on the other side of the breakwater. I pushed hard with an oar to straighten the boat. I pushed too hard and lost control of the oar and watched with horror as it slipped from its oarlock. I could see it for a moment floating by the boat, then it was gone. I reached for it. I moved to the stern of the boat looking for it. I slumped down onto the floor of the boat. I was helpless. I would go where current and wind would take me. I looked about and saw that I was headed for something, a moored boat, a large sailboat. I stood to grab hold of it as I passed. I could spend the night there. I would be safe. The form of the sailboat with its cross-like mast passed, a distant ghost of lost hope, and disappeared into the night. I cried, not from fear now but from anger. I thought about my father. He was a man possessed. I'd come too late to try to know him. I felt the boat lurch wildly. I thought everything had come too late. I heard thunder in the distance, a long roll of it. Lightening illuminated the sky for a moment. I felt fear then in full measure. I was going to die. I was certain of it.

I tried to remember my mother's itinerary. Where would she be right now? What time would it be there? I wanted a postcard from my mother. I hadn't received one yet and now it mattered. I knew Jane would pick the best and most interesting postcards with photographs intended to make me regret not having gone with her. The cards would be cheery and newsy and would contain a few words to remind me that I needn't stay with Dodge if I didn't really want to. It came to me then that Jane had been right. Dodge was all she said he was. He was worse. My thoughts shifted to my father again and I wondered if I'd hurt him. I wanted him to hurt. I wished I'd had the strength, the courage to plunge the large kitchen knife into his heart. I hated myself for wishing that. I didn't want to kill him. I didn't want to hurt him. I wanted to love him. I wanted him to love me. I screamed my confusion to the howling wind.

The storm was close at hand. I pulled on the remaining oar, using it to keep the boat stable. I don't know how long I did that. I don't know what good it did. It kept me occupied. It made me believe that something was possible. I was still inside the breakwater, no longer heading toward it, headed instead for the private beach by the lighthouse that had been converted into a home. The water got less rough as I came nearer to shore. The current's strength lessened and I realized, after I'd been doing it awhile, that my rowing was making the boat go around in circles. I made a sound I wasn't sure was in me anymore. I laughed. I looked in at the shore and made a decision. I left the boat to swim, holding on to the stern and kicking, pointing myself toward the beach and praying.

The rain woke me. It was a gentle rain at first and seemed a dream in which I was being bathed. There was a roar of thunder near my head and the rain came harder and it shook me altogether from the sleep I'd collapsed into when I reached the beach. I remembered everything and felt nothing. I wanted only to be safe. I wanted comfort. A fork of lightening illuminated the water and the beach, and I could see myself for a moment. I got to my feet and started for the road. There were streetlights there and solid footing and some sense of protection from the storm that blew with increasing force about me. I didn't know where I was going, but I knew that it would not be back to the island. I would never go back to the island.

TWELVE

I did go back to Dodge's island. I had to. I couldn't explain it. Not then. Not when I was fifteen years old. What drew me to my father was a mystery, a compulsion shrouded, I suppose, in my determination to make the summer work. I'd started something and it wasn't finished.

The night before, when I'd arrived at Sandy's, soaked from the rain, exhausted from and frightened by my journey across Middleport's harbor in Dodge's boat, I thought only of myself. My hatred for my father was at the surface of my skin. I burned from it. As I was pulled toward sleep, I reached out for the hatred and clutched it to my breast. The morning brought different feelings, and I realized as I entered the hospital later that day that my anger had already turned to something else.

Hospitals reek of themselves. All places have their own smells —schools libraries, office buildings, houses — but none so much as hospitals. They smell like what they are, places for the sick. They enforce the suspicion that they are places of death rather than life. I have always felt this. I felt it as I walked the hospital corridor that day with Sandy. I felt it especially when the old woman, escorted by a black orderly, moved slowly toward me in that corridor. I wanted to avoid looking at her but couldn't. She was nearly translucent she was so old and thin. Her hair, what was left of it, was without color. When she got close, as she passed within a foot of me, I was compelled to stare. The old woman became aware of me and looked up and took my measure and smiled. I tried to smile back but couldn't and was ashamed of myself. Her head drooped again and she shuffled on. I watched her go and heard Sandy ask which way my father's room was, and my mind returned to the reason for our visit.

"He's down the hall, that way." The nurse pointed and Sandy nodded and we moved off, looking at room numbers as we went. When we got close enough to know we were there, Sandy stopped me. "He's all right, you know. He's just in for observation."

Sandy's father had come early to the apartment to tell us that Dodge had been picked up on his beach and taken to the hospital. I shuddered with dread at the hearing of it, at the knowledge that I was responsible. I tried to store it in one of the dark places where such things seek asylum. I couldn't. When Sandy told me we were going to fetch my father from the hospital, I agreed to go. On the way she told me that Dodge had apparently gotten drunk and fallen and hurt his head. She knew I'd run away. She didn't know I'd hit him.

"This is it." She looked at me for a long moment then smiled then nudged me ahead of her.

"Hey, kid, I was worried about you." Dodge grinned at me from the chair in the corner and got to his feet.

We sat on the dock. We'd been sitting there since Sandy dropped us off. For a long time we said nothing. Nothing had been said between us at the hospital or during the ride back. Now we watched the boats and the people fishing and the gulls. Below us Dodge's skiff bounced lightly. It had been brought back by the fisherman who'd found Dodge, and it appeared none the worse for wear.

"I hit my head on the piano. I got sleepy and fell off the bench and hit my head on the piano." He laughed. "That's the first time that ever happened. It's not the stupidest thing I've ever done, but it's a first."

"I hit you."

"I know you hit me. I can still feel it. You pack a mean right hand." He looked at me. "But it didn't have anything to do with my going to the hospital. I hate those places.."

"I hit you."

"I said you did."

"I meant to hit you."

"Okay."

"I just want you to know that I hit you and wanted to."

"Okay, I know."

He was angry. So was I. I felt it welling up inside me.

"I wanted to kill you."

"Okay, you wanted to kill me."

"I'm not sorry I hit you."

"I understand."

"Do you?"

"I heard what you said to me last night."

His admission brought the conversation to a moment of reflection.

We made our way to the Dock Cafe, which sat perched at the end of the dock that faced fast into the inlet. It was empty when we entered. We sat in one of the two booths that faced the water and Norman, the owner, came out of the back room.

"Heard you had an accident." Norman put the box he was carrying behind the counter and looked up at us. "Heard they took you to the hospital?"

"Hit my head. They took me in to see why it didn't do any damage." He smiled quickly at me. "Give us two large Cokes and a large order of fries, Norman, and hold the grease."

Norman muttered an obscenity and set about the task, and we returned to our vigil of silence. I concentrated on what was outside the window, the water and the boats and the tip of our island with its salt grass and scrub trees and rocky shore.

"What are we going to do?" He asked.

Dodge asked the question again as we walked along the small beach that fronted Conway Street against the harbor. It was private beach and most of it belonged to Mrs. Conway and few were welcome on it. Dodge never considered for a moment that he wasn't one of those few.

"What are we going to do?"

"I don't know."

"You can do whatever you like. I'll scrape together the dough to send you to your mother, wherever she is over there."

"I don't know."

"I could tell you I won't drink anymore."

"Is that the truth?"

"I don't know. I don't think it's the point. I can stop or cut back for the rest of the summer, but it wasn't the booze that made me do it. It was me. It was what I was feeling."

"What were you feeling?"

"That you were suffocating me."

"Like I felt when I hit you."

"Like that."

"Why didn't you hit me back?"

"I almost did."

"How do you feel now?"

"I don't know. My head hurts. I feel tired. I'm angry at myself. I'm sorry. How do you feel?"

"Mixed up."

"I'm not telling you we won't have any bad moments, but there will never be another night like last night. I can promise that."

"No more drinking."

"I won't promise that. But I won't get drunk anymore this summer."

"Then I won't hit you anymore."

"That's a relief."

"I don't know if I want to stay."

"Sandy will take you for a few days while you're deciding."

"I like Sandy. Do you go to bed with her?"

"You already asked me that."

"I thought maybe you'd give me an answer this time."

"What does it have to do with anything?"

"Nothing."

"Yes, I sleep with Sandy. We sleep with each other."

"I knew it." My smile was genuine. "She likes you. We talked about you. She definitely likes you."

"Maybe you shouldn't stay." He smiled and let it fade.

I shrugged and scooped up a rock and threw it out into the water. I watched the ripples. "You want to build a castle?"

The sand was hard once we got a few inches beneath the surface. It was wet and dense with pebbles. I set the oval that would be the moat, and Dodge followed me, making it deep enough for the water to seep in and stay. Together we built the wall around it, knowing as we did that the first of the incoming tide would invade our work and destroy it. We started on the castle's foundation.

"Remember the chemistry set you brought me?"

Dodge nodded that he did.

"Why didn't you come for my birthday?"

He shrugged.

"Why didn't you come the year before?"

He shrugged again. "It's hard to explain."

"How come you stopped coming to see me at Christmas?"

"What the hell is this?"

"Twenty questions."

"I don't like it."

"I don't like it that you didn't come."

"It just worked out that way. It's hard to explain."

"Remember the weekend we spent together when I was little? When you were still living with us?"

"No."

"I was five years old. It was the only time I ever really remember being with you."

"I don't remember it."

The sand castle was taking shape. We worked at opposite sides of it, trying to fashion turrets.

"You said I could do whatever I wanted to."

He shook his head.

"We went to the zoo and the movies and I had as many dishes of ice cream as I wanted. You took me on the subway. We went to Central Park. I remember the statue of Hans Christian Anderson. You said he was a great story teller and that the world needed all the story tellers it could get."

"Sounds like we had fun." Dodge's tone of voice suggested his displeasure with the subject.

"Mother went to Boston that weekend to see Uncle Ralph. You remember?"

Again he shook his head.

"You let me stay up as late as I wanted. You read me a story about a rabbit."

"I did not."

"Then it was a kangaroo."

"I didn't read any story."

"You always read me stories."

"I never did. I hated reading you stories. Your mother did it. She's the one who read to you."

"It must have been about a pelican."

"It's just not so."

"I remember."

"You remember nothing. There is nothing to remember. I didn't do much of anything for you to remember. I was a poor excuse for a father. I still am."

"You used to put me on your knee and bounce me up and down and sing, *Horsey get your tail up, tail up, tail up, horsey get your tail up, up in the air.*"

"Never. I never did."

"You used to do something funny with your hands. You locked your fingers together and went, 'Here's the church and here's the steeple, open and it up and see all the people.' "

"I left you." He screamed at me. "Don't you understand? What you said last night was true. I ran out on you."

"Why?" My question was whispered.

"I just did."

"Why?"

"What difference does it make now?"

"There must have been a reason."

"Nothing that concerns you."

"Who does it concern?"

"Your mother and me."

"I was alive then. A person. I saw things and heard things and felt things."

"It had nothing to do with you."

"You mean I didn't count."

"You were a baby."

"I was five."

"I left your mother, not you."

"You left."

"Her."

"Us."

"I didn't leave because of you."

"Me."

"All right. I left because of you too."

"I want to talk about it," I said.

"I don't," he answered. "Is it important?" He answered his own question. "Okay, we'll talk about it." We started on the castle again. It made it easier.

"I know a lot about broken homes," I said finally. "Jane has taken great pains to make me feel at ease with the fact that I come from one. She likes to deal with a thing face on by announcing her intention to do so then avoiding it. I went along with her. I suppressed my anger, my feeling of inadequacy, my hatred, as all good children from divorced parents are supposed to. It gets explained and then everyone is supposed to live with it. Everyone did. You found your island and Jane found Horace."

He stared at me.

"All these years I've been trying to figure out what's inside me. I've tried to pull it out and keep it in at the same time. I'm tired of not knowing what I feel or how I feel. I'm tired of not being able to deal with it. I don't want to keep living like this. I want to settle it. Do you understand?"

He nodded.

"You left because you couldn't stand being a father any more than you could stand being a husband."

"True."

"And all these years you stayed away because that feeling never changed?"

"It changed. It wasn't really true even at the time. It was what I thought was true. I did what I did because I didn't know how to do anything different. Then it became the way of things. It became the way of things forever."

"It's not that way anymore."

"Alison, I'm not sure I can do anything to help you. Not in a summer. Maybe not ever."

"Because you're a basket case yourself?"

"Yeah, because I'm a basket case myself."

The water washed in on the shore and broke over the front wall of the castle and knocked it down.

THIRTEEN

Climbing to our seats in the bleachers, I had the sensation of being on the side of a mountain. I closed my eyes and climbed the steep steps carefully and slowly, imagining that I was with my Sherpa guide and that I would be the first fifteen-year-old to successfully scale Mount Everest.

"You all right?"

"Yes, noble and trusted friend," I responded, feigning as best I could to my imagined lack of oxygen. "Weak though I am, I will finish this climb. I will stand by your side when we plant the flag and look out with you across the face of the globe from this pinnacle of mankind."

"What the hell are you talking about?" Dodge was looking down at me from a dozen steps above.

"I'm coming. I'm coming."

When we were seated and I could look out across the expanse of Fenway Park, a wave of excitement swept through me. I'd never been in a stadium. I'd never experienced the sensation of enclosure in such a massive structure. There were with us no more than a thousand of the more than thirty thousand who would eventually fill the place, and they were scattered about like pinheads, tiny dots, some so far away that only the empty seats around them gave evidence of their presence. It was breathtaking. It was what Dodge said it would be — a great and wonderful adventure.

There were people working below on the field and a few players were throwing balls back and forth. These, Dodge explained, were the pitchers warming up. An umpire was talking to a man in uniform who was too old to be a player. Fenway was filling up. The trickle built to a flood and the feeling of excitement grew. Vendors began screaming about programs and yearbooks and ball caps and beer and orange drink and hot dogs.

"What do you know about baseball?" Dodge licked foam from a paper cup of beer. On his head was his old beat-up Red Sox ball cap. He'd gotten it out that morning and dusted it off. "They never lose when I wear it," he said by way of explanation. Now he looked at me and waited.

What did I know about baseball? I grinned my best silly grin at him. "Do you know anything at all?"

I shook my head and he sighed deeply and began. I nodded as he spoke and listened intently and tried to understand. Some of it seemed simple, some seemed needlessly complex. But I understood that there were two teams with nine men on each. The team on the field with the gloves on their hands was the defense and the team that sent one man at a time to stand at the rubber plate with a bat in his hand was the offense. One of the men on the defense was called the pitcher. He stood on a mound of earth that made him higher than everyone else and threw the ball to the man with the mask who was called the catcher. The man with the bat attempted to hit the ball before it got to the catcher, and sometimes succeeded. That was called a hit. But sometimes the man with the bat made an out. He hit the ball to someone who caught it or picked it up and threw it to first base before he could get there or he swung at, and missed, three pitches. Sometimes he got four balls and walked to first base. When the offensive team got three outs, they changed places with the defensive team. Runs were scored when someone on the offense made their way around all three bases and arrived back at home plate without being out. The team with the most runs scored after switching back and forth from offense to defense nine times won.

This was my understanding of my father's explanation. I was pleased and he was pleased, and he told me it would be easier to learn the rest as the game went along. "If you have any questions just ask."

"Somebody will answer them." It was said by the enormous man with the big face sitting behind me. Dodge raised his cup of beer in response to the offer and I smiled my thanks and we turned back to the business at hand. It was getting close to game time.

On the way up in Dodge's truck he explained about the Red Sox and the players and how they had trouble winning pennants, and when they did win them, how they then had trouble winning the World Series. He told me about the Sox of '49, his favorite team of all time. The amazing Zeke Zarilla was in right field. Dom DiMaggio,

Joe's eyeglass-wearing brother, was in center. Ted Williams, the incomparable, was in left. He told me about Birdie Tebbetts and Johnny Pesky and Bobby Doerr and the down-to-the-wire finish that year with the Yankees and the incredible catches Zeke made in right field. Extraordinary catches they were, bringing fans of both persuasions to their feet time after time. The Yankees won.

There was another cup of beer and an orange drink and a hot dog for me. I had another half dozen hot dogs before the game was over and they were the best. The national anthem was played and the game got under way.

The Boston Red Sox and the New York Yankees. It was a mid-season game with all the drama and passion of a playoff. Fenway was filled. The short left field loomed heavenward, tempting muscular men to best it, a seductress that defied giants. The Red Sox took the field and the roar was deafening. There were many good players on the field that day, but there was only one Yaz. The man behind me said that Carl Yastrzemski came from the potato fields of Long Island and that he'd kept alive the tradition of Ted Williams and that he was, in his way, as good as any player who'd ever put on a uniform.

That afternoon was one of the great ones of my life. I remember it as entertainment, as a kind of Greek drama, with us as chorus, in which the force of good prevailed, but only after near tragedy. The game was won in the last inning when the Yaz hit a single and drove a man home. Everyone at Fenway was on their feet. In that moment, with the smell of peanuts and beer and hot dogs, with the roaring of the crowd, with the cramped running of a tired and pain-ridden man to first base, I understood baseball. I looked at my father and saw on his face a moment of unfettered joy. He was shouting and waving his ball cap and it made me feel wonderful to witness his pleasure. Then I started screaming myself.

FOURTEEN

The summer was more than half over and the days started passing faster, as though they were sliding down a hill rather than climbing up one. We worked a few days a week and played the rest, fishing, swimming, driving off to some place or other because Dodge thought or I thought it would be interesting. We took the ferry to Block Island and spent a day there and drove over to Newport another day and went to the old Vanderbilt mansion and walked about it and pretended that it was ours, that he was Vanderbilt and I was heir to all. It was a grand game that we both relished and both played well.

I got caught up in Dodge's life as it was before me, as it would be without me after I left. One day there was a note in the mailbox from Mrs. Conway. She wanted to see Dodge, and he brought me along. He dressed carefully and told me to be my most gracious as we walked along the street that bore her name and came finally to her house. Mrs. Conway was a woman of breeding, a woman in her eighties who had some money and who once had a great deal more. Her house and the island were the vestiges of that position. She was a woman of great bearing and graciousness, and it came to her naturally. She was interested in Dodge and me and the house and her island and she served tea and it was very pleasant. Afterward we got to business. Mrs. Conway's children wanted to sell the island. They wanted Dodge off and the island sold. There were at least two prospective buyers and the sum of money was substantial. Mrs. Conway did not want to sell the island, but while she didn't mention it, the pressure upon her to do so was great. She had in mind to leave the island to the village of Middleport when she died. She wanted it to remain a refuge for animals and wild things. She wanted Dodge to continue to live there, but she could not ensure that possibility, even for another year. That was the purpose of the conversation finally. She wanted Dodge to know that he ought to start looking for another place to live. One day soon she suspected he'd have to go, and she wanted him to be prepared. He thanked her and we left.

I looked at the island and our house in a new way when we returned. I saw it as something inseparable from my father and I was angry. He consoled me. He told me that he always knew it would happen. His arrangement with Mrs. Conway had always been that she had the right to evict him at any time. He understood her predicament and was grateful that it had taken as much time to happen as it had. He could afford something else now.

"Maybe I'll take a place in town," he said. "It's been so long since I could just walk somewhere for something. It might be fun."

I couldn't believe it. I protested. How could he give up his island.

"It won't happen for a while yet," he said.

On another day I rowed back to the island from errands in town and saw a boat tied to our dock. I decided to play a game. I would dock quietly and sneak up on the house, an invader, a spy, a patriot performing a service for her country. It was all so easy. The dock was far enough away to tie up without being heard. The house could be approached in so many ways that I had only to pick one. I moved down the beach away from the house, then back into some scrub trees and around to the back, past the outhouse, finally to a window. I looked around then carefully raised my head until I could peek in. Dodge and Sandy were making love in his bed. They were at a point of intensity that caused them to thrash about and hold onto each other. I had never witnessed lovemaking before, and the emotions I experienced in doing so were many and confusing. I was repelled by it and fascinated by it and felt a strange sensation within me that was both desire and disgust. I watched them when they finished, lying side by side, talking to each other gently, touching each other, kissing a few times. They were very tender with each other, and I felt the sensation of something else. I watched as they cared for each other and felt myself tingle and realized they were in love, that I was watching love. Sandy pulled the cover up after a while and they snuggled beneath it. I made my way back to the dock, back to the boat and rowed out into the harbor.

Images of Sandy and my father swept over me. The time Sandy and I had spent together that summer were relived. That I had gone to her when I'd run away was an action taken without thought. There was nowhere else for me to go. We had become friends because of it. She'd comforted me. She'd talked to me about my father, about her and my father. She'd been honest about it to the point of tears, hers, then mine. That I went back to him was at first as much her doing as mine. When I went to him at the hospital, it was with a sense of strength and understanding I'd not had before.

I stopped by the hardware store as often as I could after that. When it was a morning, we'd go to the diner for coffee and talk. She told me about her life and I told her about mine. She told me about her childhood, about Middleport when she was fifteen. We talked of men and boys and the future. Sometimes she'd talk about Dodge. She wanted him different than he was and saw no signs that it would ever happen. I tried to explain him, what I thought I knew of him, but never felt I did it well.

There were things Dodge and Sandy and I did together. We went to the public beach once, but the crowd made Dodge unhappy and we never returned. We went out in the boat together, sometimes fishing, sometimes just to picnic and swim. We went to the movies and out to dinner and once took a drive to Watch Hill to see how the rich lived. I felt awkward there, listening to Dodge's descriptions, knowing, as he knew, that he was talking about the same people I knew in New York. Sandy became my friend. My first adult friend. Now I thought about what I'd seen, wondering how I'd feel when I saw her again, wondering what it would be like to make love, to feel that warmth, to share that moment with another human being.

When I returned to the island, Sandy was gone and Dodge was having a drink. After a few minutes of conversation I retreated to my loft. Maybe they'd seen me watching. Maybe it was just my imagination. The next day everything seemed normal, but I couldn't get the picture of them out of my mind.

"What do you think?" Dodge stepped back so I could see. He studied the work himself then turned to look at me. I squinted at the sheet of plywood that had been painted white, that was reflecting light in my eyes. I moved closer to it and walked a bit to the right, then a bit to the left, making the pronouncement of my judgement a matter of great weight. I found myself finally standing next to my father.

"Nice," I said.

"Nice?"

"Nice."

"Nice isn't so hot."

"There's nothing wrong with nice."

"I didn't say there was. It's just not what you'd call a strong reaction."

I studied it further. "It's definitely nice."

We stood side by side and studied the clam on the half shell that Dodge had painted in the upper right hand portion of what would eventually become Mr. Abruzzi's sign.

"Is it large enough?" he wanted to know.

We both pondered the question. He'd painted a number of signs over the years, but none that required this degree of freehand artwork. Mr. Abruzzi was an important test case, and since he was paying money, good money, the test had better be successful. To cover his bet Dodge had made the whole thing very large and very garish. The sign would be above the entrance to Mr. Abruzzi's place, and it would be big and colorful so as to obscure any deficiencies resulting from its creator's lack of talent. The question at hand was, was the clam big enough? Was it big and bold and impressionistic enough to cover the fact that close up it looked like a lousy clam, in fact, hardly like a clam at all?

"How big do you want it?"

"I don't know. How big do you think it should be?"

I started backing up again. "I think it should be bigger."

"How much bigger?"

"About three times bigger."

Dodge started immediately for the paint. "I'm going to make this the biggest clam you ever saw." He dipped the brush into white and started to obliterate the clam that was so he could begin work on the clam that would be. I watched.

"You and Sandy going to get married?"

"Ask her."

"I did."

"And?"

"She said to ask you."

"Well, there's your answer then."

Dodge outlined the clam lightly in the other corner of the sign, making it as big as he could and still have room for Mr. Abruzzi's name.

"I think you should do the clam gold."

"Clams aren't gold."

"You're not making a clam, you're making a sign. Gold is good for a sign."

"Just so happens I have gold."

"I know. That's why I suggested it."

"Well, stir it up and get it ready and clean those brushes."

"Yes, sir." I saluted and did as I was bid, and we worked together for a time in silence.

It was a cool day for August. A rare day that brought with it dry, fresh wind to touch the skin, to make you feel that, while time may have carried on in other places, here, around you, it was standing still. I have had that feeling often and I relish it. Each time I feel that sensation, no matter where I am, that day in August comes to mind. It was a day to smile and a day to ponder. It marked the beginning of the end of our summer, and somehow I suspect we both knew it.

I had irregular meetings with Tommy Raymond at the drugstore and continued to encounter Auggie Sinclair in town and continued to be embarrassed by his outbursts. I went with my father to do another job for Miss Nicholson and one day went to talk with Mrs. Conway, who was getting into a car to be driven to church. I went to church one Sunday to see what it would be like. Dodge wouldn't go with me. Saint Michael's minister, the Reverend Barnard, was on vacation, and the crowd for his replacement was small. The sermon was short and to the point. It dealt with maintaining a moral stance in a world that no longer seemed to care about such things. He was a nice man and said hello to me as I left.

Dodge and I spent our days talking and taking walks about the island. He wouldn't talk about the prospect of his having to leave his house and chose instead to concentrate on my future. His interest in where I wanted to go to college and what I wanted to do with my life increased with each passing day. I couldn't answer his questions and it became a kind of game. We talked about big schools versus small schools. We compared professions and made predictions about the sorts of jobs that would be important and rewarding when I was a grown-up and needed one. We talked about the changing world and how dim prospects seemed for the individual in a society that would require greater and greater control of its citizens in order to manage them and the resources necessary to sustain life.

The time passed pleasurably, but we became increasingly aware of its passage and that put an edge on it. Almost everything we did, nearly everything that brought us happiness was tinged with the knowledge of how short our time together was. Dodge rigged a sail for the skiff and we built a rudder, but he wouldn't let me use it alone. We fought about that and he set to teaching me but still wouldn't let me go out alone. I nagged at him about it every day. At night we sang songs, his songs. I learned many of them and we did well together, singing at the top of our lungs, I'm sure driving people across the channel to their cupboards for the whiskey. We took turns cleaning and cooking and started sprucing up the house and the grounds around it. We wanted the place to look as good as it could and to hell with the future. A gradual order came into being. There was a definite routine to our lives, a definite purpose. A harmony had come into being.

"How come you and Jane got married?"

Dodge was painting dark gold ridges along the base of the clam with a thin pointed brush. His hand shook terribly until brush touched wood. Then it steadied like a surgeon's and the lines were straight and true.

"I'm glad you did because I'm glad to be here, but I never could understand how come you got married. You're the two most different people I ever met."

"We weren't always different. At least we didn't think we were. I'm the one who changed. I think she's still the same."

"Did you love her?"

"I think so. We were happy for a while. We were a cozy little family once upon a time, the three of us. Just like the three bears."

"That's a happy thought."

"It was happy while it lasted."

"Why didn't it last?"

"Me."

"It was all your fault?"

"That's simple enough isn't it?"

"She was always the way she is now?"

"I think so."

"She's not easy to live with."

"I don't want to spend the day picking on your mother."

"Well, she isn't."

"She's consistent. She's honest in her way, as honest as people get. There's no guile to her. And I suspect deep down she's a decent person. A frightened person but a good one."

"You couldn't work it out with her?"

"I didn't try. There was nothing to work out. I hated my life. She was a part of it. I changed my life and she got left behind." He stopped to look at me. "I wanted to change everything about my life. Everything."

"So you came here."

"Here."

I looked about at his house and island and back at my father. He was staring at me with amusement. "Doesn't seem like much to end up with, does it?"

"I didn't used to think so."

"And now?"

"Well, we've fixed it up a lot."

He looked at me for another moment then went back to work.

"How come I had to stay with her? Why couldn't I come with you?" I watched him paint and waited for an answer. There was none. "Didn't you want me?"

"Sure I wanted you." He stopped painting again. "That's not true. I didn't want you. I didn't want anything from that life."

"I wanted to come with you."

"How could you know that?"

"I wanted to."

"You were five years old."

"I remember wanting to come with you. I remember when Jane told me that we were going to live alone that I didn't want to. I wanted to be with you. I told her so. I remember telling her so. She just wanted to keep me for herself. She didn't care how I felt. She didn't care about me." It came pouring out, and I was screaming by the time I came to the end of it.

When Dodge finally spoke, he did so quietly. "You stayed with her because that's where you belonged."

"It didn't matter what I wanted to do?"

"A lot doesn't matter when you're five years old. A lot doesn't matter whatever age you are. It's hard for a kid to understand, but none of us gets our way very often, even if we go off to live on an island." He went back to work then and turned his back to me.

"Why didn't you work something out so I could spend vacations with you?"

"Because I didn't want to."

"Why did I have to wait ten years to spend a summer with you?"

"Because."

"What the hell kind of answer is because?"

"Because it was the first time you asked to spend the summer with me."

"I wanted to ask you before but I was afraid. I didn't want to hurt Jane's feelings. I was afraid you would say no."

"I would have."

"You didn't this time."

"I almost did."

"Why? Didn't you want me to come?"

"I did. That's why I said you could."

"You didn't want me here. You hated the idea. You wanted me to leave the minute you saw me at the station."

"You wanted to leave the minute you saw this place."

We both laughed. "I did, didn't I? It looked like a dump."

"I fixed it up before you got here. You should have seen it before that."

We laughed some more and settled into silence. I cleaned a brush and watched him try to paint the meat of the clam in its shell pink.

"It should be dark gold, with highlights, almost like a pearl."

Dodge held up his brush. "You want to do it?"

I did and he handed over the brush and sat down and watched as I started painting gold over the pink. It produced a strange color that didn't seem to work at all. I stepped back to look at it and kept backing up until I decided that a second coat of dark gold over the first, after it dried, would produce the desired effect.

"Do you love me?" I asked it with my back turned to my father.

He responded at once. "Of course I do. That's a stupid question. It's an impertinent question."

"I don't think you do. I'm not sure I love you. I'm not sure what love is."

"That's a deep subject. You sure you want to get into it?"

"Yes."

"It's not going to go anywhere."

"How do you know about love? Whether you're in it or not?"

"I don't know."

"Is it something you feel?"

"That's what they say."

"What?"

He ignored my question so I asked another. "What does it feel like?"

"What?"

"Love.

"You'll know when you feel it because it's different than the way you feel the rest of the time."

"Where'd you read that?"

"I don't remember." Dodge's smile was genuine, and it conveyed both the realization that he couldn't talk around the subject and the concern over where the discussion might lead. "How the hell should I know what love feels like? You're talking to the wrong guy."

"I feel different when I'm with Tim. Different than the way I feel the rest of the time."

"Yeah, well, don't feel too good. Wait until you're back in New York before you do that."

"Why?"

"Because it's none of my business, that's why. That stuff should happen when your mother's around."

"Why do some people think it's wrong to have sex before you're married?"

"Because they think it should be saved for special occasions."

"There are special occasions besides marriage."

"Damn you're a nosy kid."

"Being in love must be special."

"That's why it's good not to love too many people at the same time."

"I'm not promiscuous."

"You don't know what's going on yet."

"That's why I'm asking."

"That's not how to find out. You have to get experience."

"That's what I thought."

"Now wait a minute. I don't mean you have to get that kind of experience. Not directly. I mean you have to live some and be older."

"How will I learn then?"

"You don't have to know so much."

"Does it feel good?" He ignored me. "Does it?

"School's over for today."

"Does it feel good?"

"Sure it feels good. Otherwise people wouldn't do it."

"It must because it occupies so much of everyone's attention. Mother is terrified of the subject. I've never been able to have a serious conversation about sex with her. She changes the subject. She uses euphemisms for the parts of the body. Do you want to hear what she calls my ...?"

His "No!" cut me off and echoed across the island. He got up and walked a few feet away, then started to pace. He thought about leaving altogether. She was crazy if she thought he was going to deal with this. He watched her as she painted. Someone is going to get one hell of a woman he thought. She's pretty and bright and her body is going to make men covet her. He stopped himself as he felt a yearning for his own youth rise up in him with a rush. He didn't want that. He saw her stick out her tongue at him. He saw her laugh and go back to painting. She was playing, asking questions that were serious but in a way that was making it hard for him. She knew what she was doing and probably understood the effect of it on him. He was being forced to deal with things that were none of his business. He wanted to tell her that. She was still talking and he found himself, reluctantly, tuning back in.

"Mother is unwilling or unable to discuss anything about sex. I'm a normal healthy girl and I want some answers. At least some points of view to consider. Don't tell me you don't know anything about it."

"That's very personal stuff, Alison, and it's none of my business."

"I didn't ask you what you and Sandy do. I just asked in general."

"In general it's none of your business."

"I've let boys feel me up and stuff like that. But I've never wanted to make love. I'm beginning to feel that I ought to pretty soon. Try it, I mean. To see what it's like. I ought to get the first time out of the way so I know what I'm dealing with."

"Don't feel any pressure on my account. More than anything in the world I want to send you back as you arrived. Intact so to speak."

"Boys become men and that's part of their experience. No one says they can't have some understanding of their bodies and their physical feelings and have some sexual experience. I should have the same right."

"It's different."

"Of course it's different. A man and a woman are different. They have different kinds of feelings and attitudes and needs. I can read. But I want to know what the differences are."

"Just differences."

"I'll tell you what's different." I was angry now, dealing with an injustice, dealing from the strength of moral indignation. "I'll tell you what's different. What's different is that it's all right for a boy to get laid but not a girl. A boy who gets it is a big deal. A girl who gets it is a whore."

Dodge hesitated. He'd been presented with a simple truth and he wasn't sure what to do with it. The thought, so clearly expressed, hadn't occurred to him before. He tried to answer carefully.

"That's what society thinks. You're right about that. It's hard to live in society without paying attention to what it thinks."

"I've heard that one before."

"That's because it's true."

"I'm not talking about sleeping around. I'm talking about having sex with someone you like. I'm not talking about the end of the world. And before I do it I just want a few answers, that's all."

"How about a swim?"

“That’s your advice on the subject of sex?”

“It is for now.” Dodge started for the house. “I want to think about it before we talk anymore.”

“You’ve never thought about it before?”

“Not in relation to my daughter.”

I put the brush in a jar of turpentine. “Let’s go for a swim,” I said.

We swam off the boat. I rowed out beyond the island and we anchored and I dove off and waited for Dodge, who was still taking off his shirt. When he came to the surface from his dive I was waiting for him. I grabbed his head and pushed him under and held him there for a long moment then swam away for dear life. He sputtered for air then came after me. I shrieked and he disappeared beneath the surface and I stopped swimming to look for him and a moment later felt myself being pulled under from below. We played in the water until we were exhausted. We rested in the boat then, absorbing the warmth of a sun that was giving off its final heat of the day. It would be evening soon. It would be night. Another of our days would have passed, and we would be one closer to parting.

“I can’t make up my mind about a lot of things.”

Dodge grunted a noncommittal response.

“I don’t know whether I like the sunrise or the sunset best.”

“What’s wrong with liking both of them.”

I hung my hand over the side and played with the water. “When are you going to let me take the boat out with the sail?”

"When you're ready."

"I'm ready. As ready as I'll ever be without going out and doing it alone."

"Soon."

"How soon?"

"Soon."

"Tomorrow."

"Maybe."

"Tomorrow."

"Maybe."

"Tomorrow."

"Tomorrow," he agreed.

The next morning I rigged the sail and rudder under Dodge's watchful eye. He was filled with advice about how to feel the wind and how to play the sail and not to let water in over the side and to be careful, especially to be careful.

"It's not a good sailer. There's no centerboard. It will slip all over the place. Stay out of the channel."

I listened and said I'd be mindful of everything he taught me and I pushed off from the dock. The wind was right and across the beam of the skiff, and I sailed out into the harbor smartly. I turned once to wave to my father and saw him waving back from the dock. Then I returned my attention to sailing. It was a kind of freedom I'd not experienced before. To be alone in a small boat under sail was exhilarating.

Dodge watched from the dock as the boat caught the wind and pulled away. He watched as his daughter headed out into the harbor and saw her look back once and returned her wave. He saw her point the boat a bit higher and tighten up on the sail and heel over a few degrees. She'd promise to stay inside the breakwater and to come back in a few hours. He watched as she pointed higher still and started to disappear around the point toward Conway beach and the town clock. He watched until she was out of sight.

FIFTEEN

I wrote my mother once a week. I had promised that. I checked the itinerary I'd been given and mailed the letter to the place where they'd be a week later. In return I received postcards that had been selected for the beauty of their views and that contained florid descriptions of people and places and the wonderful time they were having and how unfortunate it was that I wasn't with them. For my part I kept the letters I wrote simple and direct. I wrote selectively of my summer. I omitted anything that required explanation.

I did not write that I arose each morning with first light or that I watched the beginning of each new day from my vantage point in the loft. The routine that unfolded across the channel had become personal. The activity of getting ready for a new day, the people I saw leaving houses, the regularity of their habits became a fixed part of my own getting ready. If something unusual happened or something that was supposed to didn't, I became concerned. I knew people now and thought of them as neighbors and friends. I became, like the sun itself, part of the process of getting Middleport under way.

This was Thursday morning. It was to be a work day. We were going to put in a brick walk at the Harrison place. Mr. Harrison was a retired Navy officer. He had only one arm. Mrs. Harrison was a distant woman who was pleased to see you and who always left you feeling uneasy about yourself. The walk would go from the back door to the edge of their yard, winding as it went through flower beds and shrubs. The bricks were waiting for us.

I was up earlier than usual this Thursday morning because the night before I'd put the finishing touches on a long and carefully thought-out scheme. I'd bought a spool of black fishing line and a sinker and had managed, when Dodge was out, to get the line across from the loft to the farthest beam by attaching the sinker to it and throwing it. The feat required about a half hour of missing before I connected. I secured my end of it, after lowering the sinker over the beam, to the floor below. Then I went downstairs, detached the sinker, attached what I'd bought in the toy department of the drugstore, returned to the loft, and raised it back up nearly to beam height. Now, with my face carefully concealed behind my pillow at the edge of the loft and with the light playing softly on Dodge's face, I lowered my surprise. It descended directly to my father, who was snoring spasmodically and whose hands were crossed on his chest like a corpse. I lowered the line until the object at its end brushed lightly against his cheek. Then I raised it quickly, just as his face twitched. I lowered it again and he batted at it. The third time he opened his eyes and screamed.

The huge hairy rubber spider was no more than a foot from his eyes, just in focus, dangling its quivering ugliness at him. I let go of the line and the spider fell on him and he started flailing at it and I yanked on the line and the spider shot a foot into the air and fell back to the bed again and Dodge attacked, then saw what it was.

I was nearly crushed by the weight of my laughter.

He looked up at me, took a look at the rubber spider and shook his head. "Very funny," he said. Then he laughed.

Breakfast was cold cereal and toast and coffee and a lot of complaining about what I'd done to him and a series of lurid descriptions of the various ways in which he intended to pay me back. Finally he calmed down and was able to laugh a little about it. Then he made me promise never to do anything like it again. Then he told me to check my bed very carefully each night for fear there'd be something live in there. He didn't fool around with rubber.

I rowed us across the channel and deposited a letter for my mother in the mailbox and lifted the red flag to let Charley know it was there and headed into town. We went to Bateman's to pick up bags of cement. While Dodge talked business with Mr. Bateman, I talked with Sandy. We hadn't seen each other since the day I'd caught her in bed with my father, and I was self-conscious in her presence.

"How are things out at Alcatraz?"

I played with a doorbell display on the counter. "The warden's improved some. And the food's better."

"No more riots?"

I shook my head.

"It must be nice, you and him getting along finally."

"It's more than nice."

"I wish I saw more of you."

"You wish you saw more of him."

"That too."

"That first."

She looked at me, hearing what I heard myself, a note of jealously. I think we both thought it was all right. We smiled at each other, and I'm sure a moment of understanding passed between us. It was the first time I'd ever felt like a woman. "You want to come over for dinner? The place is cleaned up."

"Well, if you can eat out there, so can I. I'd be happy to."

"Come after work."

"Shouldn't you ask him?" She nodded her head toward Dodge.

"You're my friend too."

I told Dodge about Sandy coming to dinner while we were driving to the Harrisons'. He told me I'd have to do the cooking and entertaining since I did the inviting. Then he told me that my job that morning would be cleaning bricks. It seemed an easy thing until I saw the bricks, a huge pile of them, half ready to set into the walk, half with cement clinging to them like ugly growths.

"Clean them carefully," he said. "It'll cost you a quarter from your pay for each one you break." He handed me a two-headed hammer, one end of which was flat, the other which was shaped like a chisel, and left me to figure out how to make good on his order.

Dodge marked the walk by staking it every six feet and laying line from stake to stake. He then ran slats of wood into the ground below the string, wetting the wood and bending it where the path was to curve. Then he dug the path out so that the bricks would come flush with the ground around them. He scraped and evened the ground and started laying in the first of my bricks. By then I'd cleaned up most of the pile and broken only a half dozen. I was good at it finally, hitting the bricks in the right places, just hard enough for the concrete to break loose. We continued our work through the morning without once laying eyes on either of the Harrisons.

"Iced tea if you care for it." It was Mr. Harrison holding a tray in his one hand. I took the glass greedily and accepted the invitation to sit for a moment on the back porch. Dodge drank his down thankfully and kept on with his work. Mr. Harrison and I watched him for a while. "Good worker, your father," he finally said. "Good man. I know men. I commanded three different ships when I was in the Navy. I know men." He went inside.

I worked until the bricks were cleaned and then was set free. It was a warm day and quiet at the height of it and the stores that lined Carpenter Street and Smith Street where they met were mostly empty. The canvas bag store and the art supply store had no one in them at all. The book shop had a single browser. I spent fifteen minutes looking about at Mr. Sylvester's entire stock of hardbacks and paperbacks and found something that I thought Dodge might like, a book on sailing ships. I had Mr. Sylvester put it aside and continued my wandering, waving to people, exchanging greetings with them as I went. I was known in the village now, not just as Dodge's daughter, but for myself as well. I liked feeling that I belonged.

"Alison Dodge of New York and Middleport. Daughter of Al Dodge by way of Providence, Rhode Island. Lives at Conway Island. Good day to you, Alison Dodge." It was Auggie Sinclair, and he was bearing down on me, wearing, in the midst of the heat, his wool army overcoat and wool cap and carrying a shopping bag that seemed about to burst with mysteries. "How's Alison Dodge this fine day in August?" He didn't wait for an answer. "You're looking fine and dandy, as they say. Indeed, yes, you're a fine young woman. Say hello to your father for me." Auggie said all that, more than he'd ever said to me before, and swept by without stopping, without giving me an opportunity to respond.

"My father's fine and so am I and it's kind of you to ask." I shouted it all at Auggie's rapidly diminishing figure. "I hope you're well too."

Auggie turned back toward me and studied me for a moment. "Thank you," he said. Then just as suddenly he was a retreating figure again, moving off with hurried footsteps to wherever it was that he spent time. No one seemed to know or care.

Tommy Raymond was waiting by the bridge. It was one of those days. I still wasn't altogether used to the idea, as much as I cared for it, that a walk through town meant seeing nearly everyone you knew. It was the pleasure of it and the risk, depending how you felt and what you had on your mind. Tommy offered me the secret grip and I responded and we arranged our next meeting and I moved on, making my way to Benedict's Radio and Electric, where I'd priced portable radios and pretty much decided which one to buy. I had them put it aside with my promise to pick it up by Saturday. It was something I wanted to leave behind.

When I returned, Dodge was setting the last of the bricks. I watched until he was finished.

Sandy arrived at seven. Dodge rowed over to get her and handed over a Scotch and water he'd brought with him in a mason jar. He was feeling good and kissed her at mid-channel and Sandy didn't seem to mind at all. When they arrived at the house, I was halfway through my dinner preparations, and I refused their offers of help and sent them to sit and drink outside.

Dinner came and went. It was followed by the playing of the piano and the singing of songs. We sang *There's a Small Hotel* and *Summertime* and *Stormy Weather* and *Side by Side.* Dodge performed a concert for us then, playing and singing obscure songs and some of his favorites. *Sentimental Journey* and *Sleepy Time Gal* were done with feeling. He ended with *September Song* and we all sang *Moonlight Bay* together and Dodge took Sandy home.

I cleaned up and snuggled down in bed and watched the stars from my place and picked the brightest of them and made a wish.

SIXTEEN

"It's a bicycle."

"I know it's a bicycle."

"It's for you."

I circled the freshly painted red bicycle. It was an old English racer with three speeds and an old dark brown wicker basket. The seat was new. "It's a terrific bicycle."

"You know how to ride it?"

"I think so. It's like walking. It's not something you forget."

"I got it at Pop's. Fixed it up. Thought you could use a little independent transportation."

"Thank you."

"Yeah, well, it's just a bicycle."

I rode first to places I knew. I rode the length of Conway Street, past Mr. Slater's place and Mr. Haslam's, the old man who was always chopping wood. I rode to the town dock at the foot of Carpenter, then the length of that street, then through town. I crossed the bridge that ran south on Old Route One on the way out of town, past the musty old red brick building that used to be the town hall, which was now an office building, and cut off finally onto a well-worn blacktop road that made its way back into the countryside. The road was less than two car widths wide, and its curves and hills made speeds over ten miles an hour hazardous. There were no cars this morning, and I rode alone, past houses that were in disrepair, past fields and small woods and stone walls. It was a view of Middleport that had been hidden from me, not intentionally, but because it was so far out of the way. These were the houses of the poor, mostly black people. They were small and patched with whatever could be found to do the patching, odd boards and scraps of plywood and tar paper from rolls. There was a wreck of an old car in one driveway and the wreck of a truck in another. The lawns, where there was grass at all, were brown and spotty. I saw a black woman hanging wash in her yard. Her children played around her legs, and one of them waved and yelled out at me and giggled up at the large woman who looked down at him, then at me. Two men and a boy were fixing a porch farther down the road. This boy waved at me as well and I waved back and saw him say something to one of the men and they all stopped to look at me until I was out of view. There were black and white, young and old, and all poor on this road that wound its way away from the center of town. I rode on and on, oblivious to how far I'd gone, completely absorbed with my surroundings.

"Alison Dodge of New York and Middleport. Daughter of Al Dodge by way of Providence, Rhode Island. Lives at Conway Island. Good day to you, Alison."

The sound of Auggie Sinclair's voice came from behind me. I'd ridden around the curve intent on the small house off to my right and hadn't noticed at all the smaller house on the other side.

"Long way from home."

I walked my bicycle back to his fence and leaned it there. The sight of this old man sitting on a faded canvas beach chair reading a book nearly took my breath away. He sat there in his undershirt grinning at me.

"Nice looking bicycle," he said. "Believe it belonged to one of the Grayson girls. They used to summer here back ten, fifteen years ago. Wasn't red then but I recall the basket. Must have got it up to Pop's. That's the only place you could find a thing like that these days."

I nodded a half dozen times as he spoke and continued to study him without any pretense about my interest. He seemed not to mind at all.

"I used to ride a bicycle," he continued. "Got to be too many cars. Gave it up. Trust my feet to keep me out of trouble. Come sit."

I moved into the yard, and Auggie got up and offered his chair. I hesitated and waited while he moved off to the side of the house then returned with another chair in tow. He opened it and set it down. "Take your pick." He pointed to one then the other, and I chose the one he'd just brought and we took our places.

"Reading *War and Peace*. Read it a half dozen times already in my life, maybe more. Get to be my age you get careful how you spend your time reading. Now I read what I know will please me. I keep finding new things in old books. You do much reading?"

"In school mostly." I still wasn't comfortable. I looked around, uncertain about being this close to so strange a man. I knew he was looking at me and smiling. What I felt wasn't fear, but I didn't know what I'd do if he offered to show me the inside of his house.

"Reading is salvation. Learn from it. Experience from it. Share from it. Feel from it. It's a way of participating with your spirit. Don't trust people who don't read. How do you find Middleport?"

"I like it a lot. I didn't even know this road existed."

"Most people don't. They know it's here, but it doesn't lead anywhere they're going so they don't use it. Then they forget it. Good people live along here. All poor but all honest." He laughed at himself. "Not much not to be honest about. Not much temptation. Everyone back here works at one thing or another. Everyone back here is happy to be left alone." He looked around at what he had. "Gave my house over to the state so they could take care of me. When I die they'll get paid back by selling it. How's your father?"

"He's pulling out a tree stump for some people up near Wickford."

"Like your father. Never gave anyone a moment of important trouble since he moved here. Minds his own business. Doesn't pester people. I know. I know everything that goes on. Always have. Don't pass it around though. I was born here and never set foot outside it except once. That was to be in the First World War. Went to France for that. Was away almost two years. I was twenty-six. Came back and never left."

"What did you do in the war?"

"Rode a horse. The horse that led the other horses that pulled a big gun. Don't know how I ended up doing that but I did. Better job than most, not as good as some. I got back with myself in a single piece, which was my principal objective. You're a pretty girl."

"Thank you."

"What are you going to do with yourself?"

"I don't know. I have two more years of school. Then I'll go to college. I don't know after that."

"What appeals to you in life?"

I thought about it and could only come up with, "I like people." It sounded foolish.

"People are all right as far as they go. In ones and twos they can be just fine. They behave funny in groups. They come apart real fast in groups. They can hang people and run people out of town and they can fight wars. Takes groups to do those things. You come upon one person at a time and you're likely to get along. One person at a time doesn't start a war. Sometimes one person even shares

"My mother wants me to be a professional."

"Professional what?"

"A professional whatever. It doesn't matter." laughed at hearing it expressed that way.

"Well, there are professionals and professionals. I was in New York twice, once on the way to France, once on the way back. Didn't see anything of it the first time because they were too anxious to get us over there. Didn't see anything of it coming back because I was too anxious to get home. Before I went to France I'd thought I'd be something. After the war I didn't care to be much of anything. I did this and that. You ought to pay some mind to what you really want for yourself. You don't want to end up like Dodge and me, doing this and that." He got up suddenly and started for the house.

I inspected the house more closely while he was gone. The windows were all closed and covered with thick dark curtains. Auggie went in the front door and closed it behind him. The garage, which was to the right of the house, was set back some ten feet or so from the road and was closed. The yard was small and fenced with knee-high pickets. The grass was too long. The trees that started where the lawn faded away were scrubby looking and overgrown. There were birds singing and other sounds from the woods. No other houses could be seen from Auggie's place and there were no human sounds. It was very much Auggie's world, exactly as he wanted it to be.

He came out the front door whistling, *You Are My Sunshine,* carrying a book that he held out to me when he got close enough. "It's a biography. Biography is some of the best reading you'll do. Inspiration and knowledge in there. It's important to know that you're not the only person in the world who's felt certain things and had certain things happen to them."

I inspected the worn book. It felt old. It smelled musty.

"It's about Gertrude Stein. I got it in a box of junk I picked up. Don't know why people throw away books. It's hardly been used." He grinned.

"Thank you."

"There's a woman knew what she was about. A real thinker. A real artist. A writer, you know. Now that's something to do with yourself. Be a writer. Have lunch with me?"

I nodded that I would.

"Today's bologna and cheese on white bread with mustard. The real gooey white bread. Bad for you. Terrible. I love it. And Pepsi. Ice cold Pepsi. All that sugar plays hell with your body. I love it. Suggest you never touch the stuff again. Not after today's lunch. You got time?"

We ate in the yard on an old blanket under a tree. There was more talk about books and Middleport, and there was a piece of pie that came from a box that Auggie cut in half and shared with me. The soda wasn't ice cold and the ground was hard and the bread was a little old but I didn't mind. I didn't mind at all. I enjoyed Auggie and was intrigued by him. There was no way to know his age. I could guess because of the war, but I couldn't tell much by looking at him. He had a face like a wrinkled baby. It was lined and wizened and bright and clear. He smiled without showing his teeth, but when he laughed he opened his mouth and revealed brown and yellow stubs and a couple of what appeared to be working molars and a multitude of empty spaces. He was totally unselfconscious about the way he looked and what he said and how he sounded. His accent was the strangest I'd ever heard. It was sharp and contained sounds that were not always easy to understand, especially when he got excited. By the time I left him that day I understood him as easily as I understood myself.

Riding back to the island I thought about what I'd tell my father. I wondered how well he knew Auggie and hoped he could tell me more about him. But he couldn't. He knew less than I did. Auggie was a mystery that I'd come as close to understanding as anyone presently residing in the village. I didn't know that right away. I knew only that I'd met a strange and wonderful old man.

SEVENTEEN

"White."

"Green."

"White."

"Green."

"White."

"If it's white how will I find it in the snow?"

I contemplated the outhouse for a moment then agreed. "Green it is." I pried open the top of the can of green paint and began to stir the contents. It was old paint and there was crust on top. Beneath that, it was like water. On the bottom were lumps of paint as thick as clay. It was slow and tedious and messy work.

Dodge stood contemplating Mr. Abruzzi's sign. He had taken to working on it when there was nothing else to do. No one was in a hurry about it. He studied the clam. "It's too large," he said finally.

"I don't think so."

"It's definitely too large."

"Then make it smaller."

Dodge had in fact made the clam I'd worked on even larger than I suggested. "I can't make it smaller without doing it all over again," he decided.

"Then do it over again," I snapped at him. I was unhappy with the green paint. It wasn't mixing well and it was getting all over me and my mind was somewhere else. It had been riveted upon a single thought since the night before. I'd not slept because of it.

"Maybe I can make it smaller without doing it over. I could cover my tracks by painting a halo around it. You know, like rays of sunshine or something. To set it off."

"Sex isn't as interesting as it's made out to be."

"What?"

"I said, sex isn't as interesting as it's made out to be."

He lost his interest in the sign. "What about sex isn't as interesting as it's made out to be?"

"The sex part."

Dodge mumbled something to himself then spoke shrilly. "What sex part isn't as interesting as it's made out to be?" He waited for my answer, but I could tell by his expression that he wouldn't be happy with anything I had to say.

"I had sex last night with Tim."

"What? You what?" Dodge jumped up and down like a boy who'd dropped his ice cream in the dirt. "Why'd you do that? Why'd you do that when I asked you not to? I asked you to wait to do something like that when you were with your mother. Didn't I ask you to do that? Why'd you do that, Alison? Why?"

Why indeed. Why had we driven to the edge of the town beach and parked and watched the water and listened to the radio and made out as we had on the several previous occasions we'd gone there? Tim was aroused and I felt a stirring of something inside me I'd not experienced before and he wanted to move to a more secluded place and I said yes. We parked off in the trees on a dirt road and resumed our passion. He wanted to take off his shirt and wanted me to do the same. He wanted to feel skin against skin and so did I. I told Tim that I'd been thinking a lot about sex lately and that I'd decided to have my first sexual experience with him. I wanted it this summer and with him because I thought he was special. He had a difficult time with the directness of my approach. We talked about that for a while, about how I'd violated the man's prerogative to take the initiative in such matters. It took time but we got by all that and on with what we both really wanted. We took off our shirts and kissed, and he fondled me and unbuttoned my pants and tried to get his hand down them. I helped him and we ended up naked together in the backseat of his father's car. He was embarrassed by our nakedness and admitted that he'd only done this once before and then they hadn't taken all their clothes off. I told him I'd never done it, and he gained confidence from my admission. Then I started asking him questions and touching him and he couldn't deal with that. We weren't supposed to talk. This wasn't a class on sex education and I wasn't supposed to ask questions. We were supposed to be feeling something, giving way to our animal instincts, letting our emotions control the situation and what we did to each other. We covered ourselves with a blanket and just held each other for a long time. Then we started kissing and after that we made love. It hurt and then it felt like nothing, nothing really special. Tim had an orgasm and then had trouble looking at me. He put his clothes on right away and made me do the same and brought me back to the dock. All this I told my father. I told him I wasn't sorry about what I'd done. I was quite sure that all sex would not be without feeling. I assured him that I had no intention of conducting an endless search until I found the perfect love partner. But at least, at the very least, I would perhaps find some happiness in sex with someone I loved because it wouldn't be the first time and filled with apprehension.

Dodge looked at his daughter. He didn't know what to say. He felt his heart pounding. With anger? With concern? With his own inadequacy? He didn't know. He didn't know what the hell to do. "Are you all right? I mean physically and everything?"

I assured him that I was.

"I don't think I'm the right person. I know I'm not the right person. Someone else would be better. Sandy would be good."

"You're stuck with it."

"No, I'm not."

"You're my father and I'm here and you're the only person. You're the one I want to discuss it with."

"Your mother."

"I'm not going to wait. And she wouldn't be any help. She'd fawn over me and tell me about the beastly world of men and their carnal appetites, and then she'd lecture me about my rights with respect to my own body and tell me not to do it again until I'm married."

"That's about what I'd tell you."

"Why wasn't there any feeling in it for me?"

Dodge started for the house. I followed him. "We're going to talk about this."

Dodge poured himself a drink then sat it down and looked at me for a moment that seemed to last my whole life.

"How can I talk to you about what I don't know about?"

"You can tell me how it is for a man."

"I can't."

"Don't you know?"

"Don't get smart."

"I'm sorry. I just want to find something out. I don't think it's such a devastating thing for me to have a little knowledge."

"Men tend to be greedy about sex. Selfish. They want what they want when they want it and nothing else matters. Not all men. Most, I think."

"I'd like to discuss it in a bit more depth."

"Most men spend most of their time thinking of themselves. Sexually speaking. They want it taken care of."

"They just want to come and that's it?"

"That's one way of putting it." Dodge winced at my choice of language and I regretted it. I didn't want to make it more difficult than it was. "Aren't women supposed to have orgasms too?"

"Yes. Yes, they are."

"Does Sandy have orgasms when you make love?"

He stared bug-eyed at me. "Yes, she does."

"She does?"

"Yes."

"Does she like it?"

"I believe so. Yes. She seems to. You might ask her yourself if you need verification."

"I didn't have an orgasm."

He just stared at me.

"I've masturbated so I know what an orgasm feels like. It does feel the same, doesn't it?"

"About. Yes. The same. An orgasm is better. I mean to have an orgasm in the act of sex with someone you love is better. At least with someone for whom you have feeling." He blurted it out and dove for his drink.

"Do you masturbate?"

He nearly choked on the liquid. "Yes. Not in a long time. It's not something to talk about."

"I'm quite certain there's nothing wrong with masturbating. You don't have to look ashamed."

"I'm not ashamed."

"A person should have a healthy sex life."

"I don't understand you, Alison. I've never heard anyone talk about sex like this. No one fifteen."

"I've thought a lot about it."

"You have no experience."

"I have some," I reminded him. "Besides, I don't need experience to think. I told you the other day, I don't think a person should be promiscuous, a man or a woman. But you should definitely have a healthy sex life. You shouldn't have to whisper about it or avoid talking about it altogether." I watched him trying to absorb our conversation. Some of it was even new to me. The crystallization of a lot of ideas and feelings that I'd carried for a long time —they were making their first appearance. "The thing I want to know is why I didn't feel anything. When a man is in you shouldn't you feel something?"

Dodge cast his eyes heavenward. His expression clearly asked, "Why me?" I thought he was being funny on purpose.

"I don't think it's funny, not funny at all."

He leveled his gaze at me. "I have no way of knowing how it's supposed to feel for a woman when a man's inside her. Can you understand why I would have no idea about that?" He didn't wait for an answer. "I have no idea how sex should feel for a woman except that it should feel good and make you happy."

"Tell me what it's like for a man?"

Dodge was too far into the conversation to bow out with either anger or evasiveness. He had to deal with his daughter and the subject and he had to do it as honestly as he knew how. He sipped his drink and moved to the kitchen table and sat. He tried starting several times and didn't like much the words that were about to come out. Finally he said," If I try to tell you what I think sex ought to be for a person, just in general so to speak, will that satisfy you?"

"It will for now. But I won't promise not to ask more questions some other time." I sat across from him and, with our agreement validated, waited.

“Sex should be fun. I don’t mean to put it lightly. It’s not like having a row in a boat or going for a swim. But it’s not some mysterious activity that’s only supposed to take place in the dark. It’s a natural desire and a natural function of being alive. I’m trying to say that you are absolutely right that sex should be healthy. The problem is that not everyone agrees. And there are problems. There are always problems.”

Dodge sipped his drink and reflected on what he’d said so far. He thought he was probably doing all right but that it didn’t really matter because he was committed. “Sex is an activity between two consenting people, two people who agree that that’s how they want to spend some time together. They do it because they want to. But it involves a lot more than the physical act. There are a lot of other things going on, and they’re part of feeling good or not feeling good. I sound an awful lot like a father, don’t I?” He grinned.

I nodded that he did and said I didn’t mind. I liked it. Just then a father was exactly what I needed.

“As far as the physical act is concerned, you can get yourself a book. I’ll buy it for you if you like.” He sipped his drink. “Sex should feel good for a man and a woman. There should be foreplay. You know what that is?” He continued when I nodded. “You should try to make each other feel good, do whatever it is to each other, whatever you feel comfortable doing and have done to you, whatever makes you happy. You should try to do that. It’s giving and taking both.

“I understand.” My interruption saved my father from suffocating. He’d hardly taken a breath through the whole thing. I waited for him to collect himself. "Tim put his clothes on as fast as he could."

"Tim's a boy. He was probably embarrassed and frightened. Once a boy is satisfied he usually loses interest."

"I couldn't talk to him afterward."

"You didn't try, did you? Not like we're talking now?"

"Of course I did."

Dodge could only smile. He could only try to imagine what the effect of that had been on Tim, what the effect of such an encounter would have been on him when he was that age. "What did he say?"

"He said it was time to go home."

Dodge laughed and took another sip of his drink. "The attitude of society toward men and women should be the same. You should be free to say yes or no as it suits you. You're entitled to respect and to feeling good about it. It won't always be terrific. But if you spend time with people you care about, who care about you, then I don't think you'll get into too much trouble. Emotionally speaking. There's a double standard still, and I don't know if it will ever go away. And there are people who will try and take advantage. And you can get sexually transmitted diseases. And you can get pregnant. It's a damn tricky business, Alison. Not easy for a grown-up, never mind a fifteen-year-old."

He was satisfied with himself, thinking that he was done. He held his drink and waited contentedly for his daughter's thank you.

"What about birth control?" I asked.

"What about it?"

"What do I do about it?"

"You mean now? You're not going to do it again. Not this summer. Not before you go back."

"I don't know. I'm not planning on it. But I might. I like Tim. He apologized for being such a child last night. When he left me off at the dock he told me he realized that he'd only been thinking of himself. He liked me too much for that. He said we didn't ever have to do it again. He just wanted to go out with me some more. He said if we did do it again he'd try to make me feel good too."

"Did he have anything? Contraceptive wise?"

"Of course he did."

"Well, that will have to do. I'm not taking you to the doctor or the drugstore or wherever it is you get what you need for yourself. I don't approve of what you and Tim did. But that's over. I don't approve of you doing it again. Not because it's sex. I don't approve because I think you can have an accident. I don't approve because I think you're both too young to deal with other aspects of it. I don't approve because I'm your father and you're my child and I'm not able to handle it. But that's my problem. I'm not asking you to conduct yourself to make me happy. I'm not asking you or Tim to make me any promises. What I am asking is that you be damn sure it's what you want. You. Don't be cavalier about it. It's too good and too important to have it make you unhappy."

There was a long moment of silence in the house. We just looked at each other. Then we smiled at each other, just a little bit.

“Thank you for talking to me.” I said it and started from the house to continue stirring the green paint.

“Sometimes it’s a real pain in the ass being a father.” I could still hear him when I closed the door behind me. “A real pain in the ass.”

Dodge remained at the table for a while. He finished his drink and poured himself another and tried to remember what he’d said.

EIGHTEEN

Auggie Sinclair was buried on the last day of August. They'd found him two days earlier in his overcoat in his bed. They said he died in his sleep. Gone was a fixture, a part of Middleport that was as much the character of the place as any building or street. Auggie's death was noted with comment and curiosity and not much else. Time moves on.

I was stunned by the news. I hadn't seen him but once since the day of our lunch together and that was in town. He recited the litany he always recited when he saw me and passed hurriedly with the look of someone on a mission. I heard him hurl a greeting at someone else and was hurt for a moment that he hadn't stopped to talk to me, that he hadn't shown some sign of our special relationship. Now I wept. I felt the loss of a friend, a dear and important friend. I couldn't explain it. I didn't understand at all. I simply wept.

There was no church service for Auggie. There was no church to which he belonged and no family to impose one on him. There was a burial. There was a place for Auggie in the Maple Hill Cemetery, a small out-of-the-way corner that belonged to no family, that was large enough only for a small old man. It was at the farthest end of the cemetery from the road. The grass had to be cleared away where it had grown up from neglect, and some bushes had to be removed before the grave could be dug. When it was done it was a pleasant corner. It formed an alcove that was surrounded by trees on three sides. There were no other graves immediately nearby. I could hear the birds singing, and I knew the animals would come close after we left. I knew Auggie would like that.

I stood with Dodge and Tommy Raymond and the man from the cemetery and the man from the funeral home. My father wore a necktie and had not complained once about coming or how I wanted him to appear. Tommy had come gladly. He wore a suit. He'd known Auggie for a long time. The two of them seldom spoke, seldom acknowledged each other's presence. It was as though they knew that each was special in his own way, and that they had no desire to impose themselves, one on the other. It had most certainly never occurred to Tommy to make anything unusual out of the old man who sang people's names. Perhaps Tommy saw some aspect of himself in Auggie. Perhaps he understood that one day a place would have to be found for him and he'd need someone to put him in it. I wore what I'd worn on the train when I came to Middleport.

They put Auggie in a plain board box, a kind of composite material, Dodge explained to me. It was all that could be afforded. The trip to the cemetery was made by the hearse and Dodge's pickup. The service was brief. The man from the funeral home was nearly finished. When he said his last, the box would be lowered into the ground and covered with earth and the sod would be put in place and Auggie Sinclair would be given up for lost.

I pulled at Dodge's arm and whispered loudly enough to be heard by everyone, "Can I say something?"

"What?" he wanted to know.

"I just want to say something."

"My daughter wants to say something when you're done."

The man from the funeral home acknowledged the request by continuing the service at an even faster pace. I wondered what to say. I was frightened that when the time came I'd have nothing to say at all. I looked at the box that held my friend and tried to picture him inside. I hoped that they'd put him in his coat and hat.

"Did they put him in his coat and hat?"

Dodge turned to his daughter, startled. "What?" He'd been shaken loose from thoughts about his father. He was wondering if it would be worth the effort to find out what had happened to him.

"Do you think they put Auggie in his coat and hat?"

The man from the funeral home scowled at me and kept going with the service.

Dodge conveyed his conviction that they had indeed put Auggie in his coat and hat.

The man from the funeral home said, "Amen."

We all said, "Amen."

"Did they put him in his coat and hat?" I directed it straight at the man from the funeral home.

"I believe so," he said. "I believe Mr. Dodge here asked us to do that."

I felt a shudder go through me. I looked at my father and nearly lost control. He was looking straight ahead.

"You want to say something?" The man from the funeral home was in a big hurry to leave.

"Can't he have some kind of grave stone?"

My father answered. "Maybe," he said. "We'll look into it."

"There should be more people here." I said that after an impatient silence. "More people should have come to say goodbye to Auggie. He was a nice old man. I think he was very lonely. He was my friend. I liked him. No matter what happens in my life I'll always remember him." I could feel the dryness spreading about my mouth. I could feel the lump swelling in my throat. It was all I could say.

After the burial we went to the best restaurant in town, and the three of us had a lunch in Auggie's honor. We told each other what we knew of him. I told of my picnic in Auggie's yard, and Dodge told of the cup of coffee he'd had with Auggie one day when the old man passed by a house where Dodge was working. It was a bitter cold day and Auggie had no gloves and his fingers holding the shopping bag he carried had the look of porcelain. They shared from Dodge's thermos. Tommy said his father had been on speaking terms with Auggie many years ago then suddenly it stopped. He never knew why. There wasn't much for us to share. I thanked my father for thinking of the coat and hat, and we said a prayer and worked our way through roast beef and a glass of wine each and dropped Tommy off at the bridge and went home.

In the truck Dodge told me that there'd be a small piece about Auggie in the paper and he'd try to do something about the stone. He'd ask around and see what he could do. I nodded and bit my lip and looked away and struggled to keep myself under control. Dodge saw me fighting with myself. He looked more sternly at the road, gripping the wheel with both hands.

The day grew hot. There was no breeze. Dodge was painting window trim. He said he needed to keep busy just then. I walked down to the beach and along the shore and waded out until the water licked my knees, and I walked that way for a while. I kept thinking about the burial and the men who'd lowered Auggie into the ground. I had insisted that we stay for that. I wanted to touch the box he was in, and I wanted to throw some soil into the ground after him. Dodge did the same and so did Tommy.

As I waded in the water I thought about all that and about the things that had happened to me during summer. I tried to remember the person who'd stepped off the train in June. I tried to remember the moment of my first meeting with my father and how I'd felt when I first saw him and the island and the house and my loft and I couldn't. It was another life. I was another person. I cried tears of sadness and tears of joy at the understanding of it and started to run.

"Dodge!" I yelled.

He saw me running toward him and knew in that instant what it was I was coming to him for. He held his arms out to me and we held each other and we cried together.

NINETEEN

The days of wet heat came and went, buried forever, one beneath the other. Clothing was picked from sticky skin. Handkerchiefs were run under cold water and wiped across flushed faces and hung on sweaty necks. Ice was used for everything. Faces were fanned. Constant comment was raised about the state of the season, some remembering when it was worse, some feeling in their joints the coming of the rain.

When it came, the rain washed away the terrible heat. People and places were cleansed and made fresh. The air changed. Moods changed. Sometimes the rain came lightly, like the mist. Sometimes it came in torrents. It kicked up dust and made puddles and created rivers. It came alone or with thunder and lightening.

When a storm moved on, sweet breezes and smiling faces took its place. Days were spent embracing life. Nights were spent on the porches drinking lemonade and beer and greeting neighbors who passed by in the dark. Tiredness is a gentle thing that leads to savored sleep. So a summer goes, buried finally beneath another season and lost forever then save remembrance.

The first few days of September hung heavy with the heat. It became hard to move about, then hard to breathe. Everyone shared the burden. Tempers heated with the rising of sun and stayed hotly lighted into the dark of the motionless night. There was no escape. The sky stayed a fine pale blue, without a cloud, without a trace of promise in it anywhere. People skulked and hid. Animals allowed their tongues to dangle and searched desperately for relief.

The heat added weight to time, and it became like a layer of dust on us all. We stayed on the island, swimming, dousing ourselves with well water, staying in the stone house where it was as cool as it would get. We talked some about Auggie, and filled in the letters that Dodge had outlined on the sign for Mr. Abruzzi. And we bickered. At first we weren't aware of it. He'd snap something at me about leaving a paint brush in the sun with paint still on it, and I'd snap something back about his leaving dirty clothes on the floor. We blamed each other for the heat and for not being able to sleep and for running out of ice and for not having beer or soda or whatever else it was that we thought we wanted. One afternoon when it was over a hundred in the outhouse I started screaming. I was in it and Dodge nearly broke a leg getting to me. There was no toilet paper. I heard myself screaming that at him over and over again. He was the last one to use the place and there was no toilet paper. I had a fit and he had a fit about my fit. We complained and bickered and sniped at each other until we couldn't stand ourselves.

Then it disappeared. The heat broke with a sweep of cool air from Canada. It came one night and it woke people up. I felt it and rejoiced. I awoke refreshed and watched the stars.

Next morning Middleport came alive with a celebration of the spirit. We went into town and found ourselves being smiled at and smiling back. There was music in the voices of the people who greeted each other. It was as though we'd all emerged from a hundred-year sleep. It made us laugh and we felt good.

It was a day for getting ready. Labor Day weekend was about to be observed. The band shell and the grounds around it were being made ready. The rails on the stand were repainted. The grass was cut and raked and watered. The sound system was checked and the band rehearsed. Most of the musicians had to take the afternoon away from work to do that. They were working people mostly, but a few were students and retired people, and they all gave up something to work their way endlessly through selections of light symphonic music and show music and their medley of contemporary hits. The Middleport Town Band was the source of great pride. It played a concert series about the state as well as one at home. Labor Day marked the end of their summer season.

The town beach is where the clambake was held. The pit was scooped out and the tables and benches made ready and the grounds cleaned up. Captain Matthew Worth was the man in charge. He was a man in his late seventies and he'd been bakemaster in Middleport for half his life. He'd gotten the job from his father, who'd died young, and this was, he'd let it be suggested, his last year. Captain Worth was a legend. No one in southern New England who cared about clambakes was unaware of his magic. He was small and wrinkled and his skin was permanently brown from the more than fifty years he'd spent working the water. His hands were bone and muscle and his grip was unbreakable. Today he was talking to his assistants and inspecting the grounds and making sure that his people and tools were all in working order.

The Little League field where the annual town softball game was held was dressed up with red, white, and blue bunting. There would be umpires in blue suits, and the first ball would be thrown out by the winner of last year's outstanding high school senior award. There would be ceremonies before the game and beer and hot dogs afterward. The game was sponsored by the American Legion and the money went to worthwhile causes. Anyone could play but few volunteered to do so. The game was left to the best players. It was rough and played to be won and not a place for someone simply to have a bit of fun. Dodge had played in the game for the last half dozen years.

There were other preparations being made. The town was cleaning itself up. Fourth of July and Labor Day were the two big events Middleport threw for itself. The summer art festival had become an event for outsiders and for business. The other holidays were quiet or personal or official. These were like town birthday parties. Young and old, rich and poor, those who didn't otherwise speak to each other or see each other for months, came together and enjoyed themselves.

Friday night, the night before it all began, I decided on a bath. There were three ways to do that on our island, take a swim, take a wash GI style from a pail, or fill the large galvanized tub with water heated on the stove. I preferred the latter and tried at least once a week, whether I needed it or not as the saying goes, to have one. A hot bath was hard work. I had to heat enough water on the stove to fill the tub halfway up. It took a long time, and I had to hurry because the water would cool almost as fast as I could add what I'd heated. I was going out with Tim.

The water felt good, and even though I couldn't soak my body all at once, I could bend myself into a position that allowed me to feel the warmth and relax. This would be my last date with Tim. We'd gone out several times since my talk with Dodge but had not had sex again. We'd talked about it and both admitted that we wanted it, but we both also agreed that it placed too great a burden on our relationship. Then we kissed and petted and came very close. But we didn't and we were glad. We liked each other and I knew I'd miss him. He was the first boy I'd spent a lot of time with. Sitting in the tub of water with my knees sticking out, I understood that caring for someone hurt as much as it felt good.

"You finished?" Dodge yelled at me as he approached the house.

"Almost."

"Yeah, well, shake your ashes. I need to come in."

"So come in. I'll cover myself with a towel."

I made a tent over myself, and Dodge went by without looking and started rummaging through the cabinet by the sink. "Where are you and lover boy going tonight?"

"A motel."

"I wouldn't doubt it."

"We're going to register as Mr. and Mrs. Al Dodge."

"Very funny."

"We're going to the movies."

"A likely story."

I thought about telling him that we'd done nothing since our talk but decided not to. Let him think what he wanted to think. "You going to sit around all night and drink?"

"Maybe I will. It's my business." He turned to watch me. "I'll do whatever I feel like doing."

"How long does it take to wash yourself?"

"I like to sit in the water. It feels good."

"You're really into feeling good, aren't you?"

"You're really into feeling bad."

Dodge grabbed the tools he was looking for and left the house.

When I was ready to leave for my date, he followed me to the dock. "I don't know why you stayed for the weekend. You could have gone back to New York. You didn't have to hang around." We walked single file and he jabbered at my back. "You're going out tonight and I'm sure you have plans for tomorrow and the next day."

"You want me to stay home tonight?"

"For what?

"I don't know for what. You keep talking about it. I thought I'd ask."

"What the hell would I want you to stay home for? You don't drink, you don't play the piano, and you go to bed too early."

"I'll go then."

"You bet your ass you'll go. I don't want you around here."

I let loose the line and started to row across the channel. I watched my father standing on the dock. He didn't seem to be standing quite straight. He held his drink and looked out toward me and didn't move. He stood that way until I tied up on the other side and climbed the ladder to the dock. I turned as I walked toward Tim's car and saw him there still, standing alone, his figure a frail silhouette against the fading light of day.

I was home by ten. We didn't go to the movies. We talked for two hours about ourselves and the summer and the future. At the dock we said goodbye. We'd see each other over the weekend, but there would be other people around. We kissed and I watched Tim drive away and I rowed back to the island. I could see a shaft of light breaking out from the house. The door had been left open. I could see Dodge coming toward the dock with a lantern. He was there when I tied up. He'd been drinking but he wasn't drunk. His eyes were red. We walked to the house in silence and went inside in silence and I went up to the loft. There was still a light flickering below when I started my nightly examination of the stars.

"What's wrong with you?" I asked it softly but he heard.

In time he answered. "What's wrong with you?"

"Why have you been picking on me?"

"Who's picking?"

"You."

"You've been a real pain in the ass."

"So have you."

"Maybe we should just leave each other alone."

"I don't want us to leave each other alone." I propped myself up on an elbow and leaned toward the edge of the loft. "I thought we were going to celebrate this weekend."

"Celebrate what?"

"Labor Day."

"Labor Day's for people who work."

"We work."

"Not hardly."

"We work enough to live in a palace like this."

"Cut the crap, Alison."

I moved all the way to the edge and let my legs dangle over the side. "This is a palace and you're the king and I'm the queen."

"I'm in no mood for your nonsense."

"And the village is our village and the people are our subjects and this weekend is a great feast that's being given in our honor.

"Dammit, Alison, this is a crap house on a piece of junk land in a one-horse town and I'm a bum and you're going home in three days."

"This is not a crap house."

"It's a dump."

"It's a palace."

"All right. It's a palace and you're a queen. Now go to sleep."

"If I'm a queen then I order the celebration. I declare the next three days a holiday. There will be a great festival throughout the village, and all my people shall attend and have a great and glorious time. I order it."

"Then I guess that's the way it will have to be."

"And I order you to escort me."

"You really are a pain in the ass."

"Is it a deal?"

"Yes, it's a deal."

"Then you'd better get some sleep because you're going to need all the strength you've got."

TWENTY

We stood, the three of us, Mr. Abruzzi, Dodge, and myself, looking up at the sign. It had a giant clam with golden rays of sunshine protruding form it and the name ABRUZZI'S CLAM BAR emblazoned in red block letters across the bottom of it. We were, all three of us, fully satisfied with what we saw. It looked good from the ground. It looked good enough for Mr. Abruzzi to count out the cash on the spot and watch contentedly as Dodge counted out half of that over to me. It looked good enough for him to treat us both to as many clams on the half shell as we could get down in a single sitting. It was well into the afternoon and we hadn't had lunch and we managed to consume enough of them to make Mr. Abruzzi's brow furrow. We picked our teeth and belched our way to the truck and went to Miner's Shoe Store to purchase something for Dodge by way of new sneakers. It was for the softball game.

The game was held at night under the lights. It was guaranteed a decent temperature and a large crowd and made the players feel like professionals. The two teams were drawn by lot from the group that had signed up. It was almost always the same group, though each year or so a new player snuck in, usually when a first-rate performer turned thirty, the minimum age allowed on the field. The game was taken seriously by spectators as much as participants, and it didn't matter that the players drank beer between innings while they were on the bench and that the scores always read in the double figures. The players, most of whom had bellies that dominated their profiles, did everything on the field as hard as they knew how. Many of them had been high school baseball stars. A few had played in college or in the service or on semiprofessional teams in places like Providence. One had gone to spring training with the Braves.

The rosters for this year's game hung in store windows all over town. One team was always BIG BLUE and had blue T-shirts, the other was known as ROUGH RED. This year Dodge was on the Reds. For three years running before that he'd been on the Blues. When we saw the roster in Sawyer's window he noted with satisfaction that his number was to be twenty-seven. It was what he always wore. He noted that the Blue team looked better on paper but that his team had more heart. He predicted a victory.

The Blues were a younger team than the Reds. And they had Stretch Davis, maybe the best player in town, at first. His teammates, the starters, would be:

John North – Right Field
Big Dibbs – Catcher
Leroy Vincent – Center Field
Al Haley – Short Stop
Bobby Noon – Second Base
Hal Grissom – Left Field
Mike Mack – Third Base
Marvin Lewis – Pitcher

There were another dozen names without positions listed below these. The Big Blue team would be tough.

The Reds roster tended more to experience. There were more bellies on this team. They knew more tricks. They were a who's who of Middleport beer drinkers.

Eddie Cage – Second Base
Lee Wayne – Center Field
Nicky Nickerson – First Base
Mean Gene Hammerman – Left Field
Ike Issacson – Third Base
Bert Wallace – Right Field
Mel Hanson – Catcher
Al DuHammel – Short Stop
Jimmy Leach – Pitcher

Dodge's name was included with the others that came below the starters. It didn't bother Dodge that he didn't start. He never started and didn't want to. That he'd been asked to play at all was still a source of amazement. They came up short one year, and happened to be in the diner when it was being discussed. They asked him if he was any good at the game and he allowed as to how he was and he was in. It was an emergency situation. He pinch-hit in the eighth inning of his first game and got a single and drove in a run. Next inning, in the field, he caught a fly ball for an out. The next year he was automatically included in the draw. He knew he'd be in by the fifth inning this year. It has become the routine. He was a good bench man. He could walk up cold and get a hit. He could get something started. He held his own defensively, and there wasn't anyone he couldn't keep up with in the beer department. This year he felt a growing sense of apprehension as the game drew close. He recognized what it was, the boy in him, and he was delighted.

I watched from the stands as my father, his Red Sox cap pulled snugly down on his head, his bright red T-shirt with the white 27 on it a size too small, warmed up. I was sitting with Sandy in the midst of two hundred or so people on our side. They were raising a terrible racket, yelling and talking and calling out to players and people in the stands across the way. The Blues had an equal number of supporters yelling and screaming on their side of the field, and there were another hundred or so scattered about on blankets and on the roofs of cars and trucks. When the announcement came for "The Star-Spangled Banner," it was instantly quiet. Miss Anita Rosio was announced. Sandy explained that Miss Rosio always sang "The Star-Spangled Banner" at town events. She had since she was in high school. Miss Rosio was presently pushing fifty. I watched as a plump, smiling dark-haired woman in an orange chiffon dress stepped to the microphone. She nodded and the record started playing and she sang what was a surprisingly good rendition of the song. Even more surprising, she remembered all the words.

I remembered that I had a Polaroid camera in my lap. I'd bought it with the money Dodge paid me for the sign. I started taking pictures. I took one of Miss Rosio and of Dodge's team when they lined up at the plate after being announced. I took one of Dodge spitting and another of him scowling up at me for taking the one of him spitting. I took one of Sandy and she took one of me. I started to take one of Dodge opening a can of beer but he disappeared into the dugout as his team took the field.

In the fifth inning Dodge pinch-hit and popped up and took off his hat and bowed to the opposing bleachers who were applauding his effort. I managed a picture of that. By the sixth inning the score was BIG BLUE 18, ROUGH RED 15. It was, by any standard of years past, a close game. The seventh was time for the stretch. It was a kind of five-minute break that allowed everyone to get themselves ready for the big finish. The last couple of innings usually took as long as the rest of the game because the realization that the game was nearly over for this year set in. No one really wanted the game to be over.

At the top of the seventh the Blue section rose to its feet and started catcalling in our direction so loud that Moose Morgan, the umpire, could barely be heard yelling, "Play ball." Big Dibbs was up first. He hit a dribbler toward the mound and caught Leach napping. Big pounded his way toward first, and Nickerson decided to get out of the way even though the ball was on its way to him. Anyone else but Big would have turned it into two. Big had to call time out to recover from getting one. Dodge yelled something at Big, and the next man up hit the first pitch down the right field line and nearly took Big's head off in the process. It was a clean single. Dodge threw the ball to second and it got there before Big did. They had him in a rundown and Dodge moved in to become part of it. Big started back for first then back toward second then back and forth until he was nearly out of steam. His final effort was directed toward second. He gathered himself and pounded toward that corner of the diamond, and the ball flew over his head and was caught by Dodge, who was waiting for him. Big used his last bit of strength to steamroller Dodge, who managed to hold onto the ball even as he felt himself smashed out toward left center field. The umpire yelled, "Out!" and Big made his way slowly to his feet and tried to recapture his breath. Dodge got up slowly and limped over to Big to show him that he'd held onto the ball, then hit him in the face with it. Both dugouts emptied and the fight delayed the game a half hour. Forty minutes later the game was over. BIG BLUE beat ROUGH RED 23 to 21.

Dodge was on his way to being drunk by then, and Sandy drove us back to the dock. She rowed across the channel with us and sang songs with us until Dodge went to sleep. Then the two of us talked. We spent the night talking, like a couple of schoolgirls, stretched out side by side in the loft. We talked until the dark was infused with the light that begins in some mysterious eastern place.

Sunday morning Sandy organized breakfast and we groaned our way through it when it was nearly noon. We got silly for awhile and teased Dodge about the fight the night before. Sandy wanted to go swimming afterward and I lent her my suit. It was tight and she looked sexy and Dodge couldn't keep his eyes off her. He thought we'd go rowing and have a picnic. The band concert didn't begin until evening so we had a whole afternoon to spend on ourselves. I didn't feel up to all that time on the water, and Dodge seemed not at all displeased at the prospect of being alone with Sandy. I wanted to ride my bicycle. I wanted to explore, to look at the places of my summer and to see if there were any corners that I'd missed. They rowed me to the dock and let me off and I took a picture of them as they rowed off.

I rode the length of Conway Street. It was nearly empty. Sunday was the quietest of days in Middleport, and a Sunday on a holiday weekend was quietest of all. There was no sense of urgency, no need to accomplish anything. It was a day in which one could indulge without guilt.

I rode to the town dock. The fishing boats were all in, all moored to their places, washed down and waiting for Tuesday. Several people fished from the dock, and there were several tourists taking pictures and pointing at things. The marina across the way was busier. Many of the boats had gone out for the holiday, but there were a goodly number left and some of those were being made ready for an afternoon in the bay or a party at night. They were being hosed down and provisioned and filled with fuel. Ice was being brought aboard and people were arriving and those already there were greeting them loudly. Out in the harbor were thirty, perhaps more, sailboats. In the bay beyond the breakwater were the tips of a multitude of sails. I could see part of our island. I could see Dodge and Sandy making their way toward the breakwater. I took a picture of the harbor and another of the dock and went on my way.

Carpenter Street became suddenly busy as I approached its center. The eleven o'clock service at Saint Michael's was letting out, and the stream of people that poured from the church was generously larger than usual. They moved slowly past the Reverend Barnard, shaking his hand, complimenting him on his sermon, giving and accepting a pleasantry. They stopped then to talk among themselves on the sidewalk, to exchange greetings with each other and news. A policeman kept an eye on things, helping to unsnarl the five minutes of congestion that occurred here, participating in the ritual because he knew everyone and everyone knew him. His name was Condon. He was overweight and past forty and he had no rank, no symbol on his sleeve that he'd accomplished anything in life. He had this duty every Sunday because he lived alone and liked working days when everyone else was off.

I stopped by Miss Nicholson's house to watch the people coming out of Saint Michael's and to wave to Officer Condon. He stood up straight and pulled his stomach in when I took his picture. I saw Sandy's mother and father come out of the church. I took a picture of them and one of the church steeple and heard my name being called. It came from above and the voice belonged to Miss Nicholson and I accepted her invitation.

We sat by the window overlooking Carpenter Street where we'd sat the first time I met her. She served iced tea and cookies. The cloth on the table was lace and very old and she saw me finger it and told me its story. Her great-grandmother had started it and her grandmother had finished it and both she and her mother had had to repair it. It had passed through many hands before now and she was concerned that there were none to accept it from her. Then she smiled and told me that she hadn't meant to spend her life in Middleport. "It took me near a lifetime to understand that it was all right to do that instead of what others thought I ought to do. I'm an old woman but I've found peace. Everything finally comes to its place. Each thing in its time." The light from the window by her head was soft and sculpted her features gracefully, and I took her picture during that moment of contemplation.

I rode the length of Smith Street. Only the drugstore was open and it would close early. Tommy wasn't by the bridge. An occasional car passed and there were a few people walking, but I recognized none of them. Tourists often swung off the new highway to come through Middleport. The village was a big attraction. It seemed quaint I suppose if you didn't live there. Its people probably seemed quaint. Long ago I had lost any notion of that.

I rode the side streets and on up past the grammar school and the auction house across from it. I rode to the four corners, past the ball field where last night's game had been played and on to the cemetery where we buried Auggie.

I walked my bicycle through the cemetery and came finally to the bit of land that was his. Grass was starting to sprout. I took a picture then another one to take with me, one for Dodge. I would do something about a headstone. I vowed to do that. As I left the cemetery I walked past a large stone with the name Mason on it. There was a new stone, a small white cube of rock with the name Abigail.

The town beach was crowded. The afternoon was a fine one for sunning and tide was high. The water was filled with waders and swimmers, with shrieking children and old people who did that slow, deliberate breaststroke that seemed a form of perpetual motion. The raft was crowded with kids. It was a long swim to the wooden platform on empty fuel drums that bobbed about offshore. It was a place to dive and swim and play. The beach was a patchwork of blankets and food baskets and coolers and umbrellas and folding chairs. At the water's edge sand castles were being built. Radios played a dozen kinds of music. Bodies glistened with oil and sparkled with the sand that had attached itself like sequins on fancy brown gowns.

I stood astride my bicycle at the end of the road that met the beach and gazed at the sea of people. I'd not spent much time here. We had our own beach and our own place to swim. I saw Tim with a group of kids. They were at the far edge of the beach playing with a football. I rode on.

Auggie's house was unchanged since the day I had lunch there. As I approached the front door, I expected him to open it and call out my name. The back door was unlocked, and I went in despite the posted notice that said the house was state property and that no trespassing was permitted and that it would be auctioned. I entered and moved through the matchbox of a hall into the room on the right. It was neat. It was fastidiously neat. Junk was stacked from floor to ceiling with meticulous order, and it covered every inch of wall space save the windows. There were pieces of furniture and old shoes and boxes and lamps and pieces of sculpture —horses' heads and the like —fishing gear and used clothing and paper bags and suitcases and orange crates and a baby carriage and a hundred other things that I would have had to pull out and study to identify. The room on the other side of the house was smaller and had a mattress and box spring on the floor. The bed was still made; I suppose from when Auggie had died in it. His clothes were still in the closet. There was a suit and shirt and tie all together on one hanger that had a caked layer of dust on it. There were shirts and socks and underwear on a shelf and a pair of black shoes and an old pair of high sneakers with holes in them on the floor. Next to the bed was a crate with a lamp on it. There were books next to the lamp and books scattered about the room in small piles, waiting their turn to be read, or, having been read, resting until they could be gotten back to. There were no pictures in the house. There was only the junk and the books. I picked up one and then another. They'd been read. They'd all been read. The pages had the feel of the man's fingers on them. The encyclopedias, the biographies, the books on economics and science and politics, the novels, they'd all been read. There was no dust on them. They felt warm. The book on top the pile by the lamp was *War and Peace.* It had a marker sticking out from its middle. I stayed a long time at Auggie's house that afternoon, and when I left I took something of it with me. I took the marker from the book he'd been reading. It had a quotation from the Bible printed on it. The printing was faded but legible in the light that flooded in when I opened the door. It was from Ecclesiastes.

"To everything there is a season, And a time to every purpose under the heaven." I read each line until I came to, "A time to weep, And a time to laugh; A time to mourn, and a time to dance." I stopped there.

Dodge watched Sandy as she napped in the sun. They would have to leave soon. It would take several hours to row back to the island, and that would leave little time to get ready for the concert. The afternoon had been the best they'd ever spent together. It was the first time he'd ever felt completely relaxed in her presence. He'd dropped his guard. There was no anger in him, no defenses set up about him. He liked the feeling. He liked the long silences. He liked the walk they'd taken about the small island where they'd gone to picnic. They made love afterward. They talked about the time after Alison would be gone, the time when they'd be alone again. Sandy would miss his daughter and he was affected by her sense of loss. He realized then that he thought of the three of them as a family. He realized that he liked the sense of that, the completeness of it. He watched her now as he nudged her gently and kissed her.

"We have to go." He whispered it.

"I don't want to."

"It's late."

"I don't care. I don't ever want to leave here." She sat up and stretched and smiled at Dodge. "I want this afternoon to last forever."

"We can recreate it."

"No, we can't."

"We can have others like it."

They looked at each other, each knowing what was held inside.

"We can try." Dodge stood and began to gather their things.

The concert started at dark. It was a good concert, the last of the year, and played with the feeling and passion of people who knew it was a final performance. Toward its end the music slowed. It spoke with the voice of nostalgia about the summer that had passed. It was the end of another season. It was a time to weep and a time to smile.

TWENTY-ONE

The notion of the clam bake came from the Indians. It was a gift, given or taken, that the settlers of New England refined and polished over the years, but one that remained unchanged in its essentials. What Captain Worth had mastered was a Rhode Island version of that New England tradition. As bakemaster he had the responsibility to oversee the ceremony and to pass on the knowledge of it to another so that his place could be taken and the tradition preserved. It was not a simple process, though it seemed so.

The soft-shell clams that were used had to be of certain size, about two inches was best, and there would be no chicken. That was a peculiarity of Rhode Island bakes. The digging of the pit, its depth and size, were as carefully scrutinized by the captain as the selection of what would go in it. A layer of large stones, smooth and round and about a foot in diameter, had been laid in. So had the firewood which Captain Worth now ordered burned. It was lighted and watched as it flamed, then burned down to embers, until the stones beneath were white hot. Then the embers were removed with old clam rakes and pitchforks and potato diggers, and the rocks were swept clean. All that took something over an hour.

The area above and around the town beach was filled with tables and benches and blankets and chairs and people. The drinking of beer and soda, the chatter and game playing, had already begin. Families and friends moved about, drifting near the pit from time to time to nod at Captain Worth, not daring to do more than that unless invited, deeply disappointed when they were not, collecting together in small knots afterwards to talk with anticipation about what would be forthcoming from the pit they could not peer into. I talked to the captain out of ignorance, and he seemed delighted to share what I asked for. He let me stand near the edge of the pit to see, then let me watch from a greater distance than that as rockweed was put in on top of the rocks and the clams on top of that. Another layer of rockweed was added and on that went the white potatoes and sweet potatoes and sweet corn and blue fish that had been wrapped in cloth and small sausages and finally whole lobsters. A canvas was laid over it all and secured about the edges with large stones so that no steam would escape and finally more rockweed was put on top of that.

Dodge watched his daughter from the table where he and Sandy and sometimes Tommy Raymond were sitting. Alison was happy. He took pleasure in that. He watched as she shook hands with the captain and went off to talk with Tim and some of his friends. She seemed to him more mature than those other young people, more assured, even though they were older. He felt he was being looked at and turned to see Sandy staring at him and smiling. She held up the dish of tomatoes and onions and cucumbers, and he took some and washed it down with beer. It was Monday, Labor Day, the last day of their summer.

Chowder was served along with clam cakes, and I heard a yell from the table and ran to it. The four of us layered oyster crackers on our chowder and devoured our clam cakes and announced that we were stuffed and couldn't eat another thing. Then the clams from the pit, a large tin dish for each table, arrived and we were forced to reconsider. The clams were dipped into melted butter and eaten whole, except for the snouts. Again we announced our condition as full to the armpits, just in time to have the clam remnants cleared and the rest of the bake set down. It came all at once, the potatoes and corn and fish and lobster. And it was all eaten, eaten until we thought we'd fall from our benches, until we thought it impossible to breathe. There was just barely room for the watermelon that followed.

For a long time after returning to the island we were content to say and do nothing. I packed my things quietly, not wanting my father to know I was doing it. I cried while I packed and didn't want him to know that either. My train would leave early in the morning. We both wanted a fast goodbye and it pleased my mother, whom I'd talked to on the phone, that I would be back by afternoon. She and Horace were eager to see me, eager to tell me about Europe, eager to give me my presents. I tried to be cheerful when I spoke with her and thought I was. The weekend was nearly gone. It had flashed by. It had cheated me, moving at a pace I desired only for the unpleasant parts of my life. When I finished packing and came down from my loft, Dodge was at the table. He seemed fixed to it. I'd seen him there so many times, in that same chair, his arms resting in front of him, his head cocked as thought anticipating a surprise, that I supposed it would be my strongest visual memory of him.

"This has been the best weekend of my life." I pinched his nose and laughed because it gave me something to do that wasn't sad.

"Me too," he said, making the beeping noise a nose makes when it's squeezed.

"I want to go out in the boat."

"It's getting dark."

"Then I want to go out in the boat in the dark."

"I wish you were twelve years old," he said. "I wish you were five again."

We rowed in silence as light turned gray and gray became infused with pink and gold and purple until dark finally snuck up on us.

"I don't want you to go back." He rowed slowly.

"I don't want to go back."

I could see the outlines of houses along Conway Street. I could see lights in Mrs. Conway's house, and I wondered what would happen to my father's island.

"I'll miss you."

"Maybe I can come up for Thanksgiving."

"We'll have it on the island like the Indians and Pilgrims used to."

"I'll be an Indian."

"I'll be a Pilgrim."

"What about Sandy?"

"She can cook."

We both laughed and accepted the silence. We accepted it gratefully then felt its impact. It became like the eye of a storm, a great heavy weight that would drag us to the bottom of the bay. My mouth was dry and Dodge's voice cracked when he spoke again. "How many songs do you know?"

"More than you."

"Not likely."

"How much?"

"Loser buys breakfast."

"It's a deal."

We shook on it.

"You go first."

"I'll start, then you sing with me." I thought for a moment. Dodge had taught me many songs over the summer. I realized that there was only one I wanted to sing. I didn't start at the beginning:

"We were sailing along on Moonlight Bay,
We could hear the voices ringing,
They seemed to say – You have stolen my heart,
Now don't go 'way' – As we sang Love's Old Sweet Song on Moonlight Bay."

Also by Michael de Guzman

Searching for a Place to be

An old, abused dog runs to save herself. A thirteen-year-old-boy witnesses a murder and runs for his life. A combat veteran hides from the world and himself. This is the story of how these three come together in a forest in the northwest, and what they do to help each other take their first steps back out into the world.

Cosmos DeSoto and the Case of the Giant Steel TEETH

In the real world Cosmos DeSoto is a twelve-year-old boy who lives with his mother, Viva. When he's not at school, he helps her with the catering business she's desperately trying to keep alive. When he's not doing either of those, he's buried in his imagination, leading his other life, that of Cosmos DeSoto, private detective. When Viva is hired as a last minute replacement to provide food for the crew of a movie, Cosmos is off on his greatest adventure. While he works with his mother on the real film, his imagination takes him into the fantastic world of the movie, TEETH, when the star hires him to protect her life.

Growing Up Rita

Growing Up Rita is the story of twelve-year-old Rita Martinez, who was born in the United States, and her mother, Alicia, who came here illegally. When Alicia is picked up in an immigration raid, Rita must find the courage and the resources to survive while she searches for her mother and tries to get her back.

The Bamboozlers

The Bamboozlers was originally published by Farrar, Straus & Giroux. It has since been translated into German (*Die Schalwiner*). It's the story of twelve-year-old Albert Rosegarden, who is bored with his life and constantly in trouble. Until the day he meets his grandfather, Wendell, for the first time. Wendell is a man with a dubious past. Albert is charmed. The pair travel to Seattle, Washington, where Albert becomes a partner in his grandfather's elaborate scheme to settle an old score and con a con man who has it coming.

Beekman's Big Deal

Beekman O'Day has lived every minute of his twelve years in Manhattan with his father, Leo. He's attended nine schools and resided in apartments, hotels, and rented rooms. Now he's got to move again, and start a new school. But this time, as they move to Nutting Court, and he begins the year at Chance Academy, his father tells him it's different. They make a deal. A big deal. Beekman doesn't want to move anymore. He wants to stay in one school. His father promises. When it seems that the promise can't be kept, Beekman stands his ground. This is the story of a boy who refuses to give up.

MELONHEAD

Sidney T. Mellon, Junior's head is round and much too large for his pencil thin body. A cantaloupe comes to mind. So does the name, Melonhead. What chance does he have looking like this and yo-yoing between divorced parents? No wonder he gets on a bus and heads for, "As far away as he could get." So begins a journey of self-discovery that takes him from Seattle to Los Angeles to New York to a small town in Rhode Island.

michaeldeguzman.com

CPSIA information can be obtained
at www.ICGtesting.com
Printed in the USA
BVHW030810220221
600773BV00004B/15

9 781505 388855